BB 299 X

FINS & CHROME

FINS & CHROME

E. John DeWaard

ARLINGTON PRESS

This edition published 1990 by
Arlington press
130 Arlington Road
London NW1 7HP

Produced by Bison Books Ltd
Kimbolton House
117A Fulham Road
London SW3 6RL

ISBN 1-871378-68-0

Printed in Hong Kong

Reprinted 1992

Contents

Chapter I. Denied, Deprived and Depraved

Long ago and far away, there was a carefree time in US history. It was the era of the malt shop, blue suede shoes, the drive-in movie, and pony-tails. It was a time when Rock and Roll was really Rock and Roll, when a house in the suburbs and a 2-car garage was the ultimate and cost 15,000 dollars. It was a time when everyone was young and Americans had a great love affair with the automobile. It was Camelot! It was the Fabulous Fifties!

If the Romans had their chariots and the royalty of another age its gilded coaches, neither of these will ever surpass the great automobiles of the 50s. For in that decade, after a long dark period, America celebrated its youth, prosperity and vigor with an automobile. They were vivid, these cars. Never to be forgotten in their glowing colors and chrome. Never to be equaled in their speed and luxury. They were brilliantly innovative with automatic transmissions, torsion bars, powerful engines, power steering, power brakes, (the country was power-mad) and air conditioning. What was more, they were fun to drive—even easy to drive!

If anything symbolizes the cars of the 50s, it is the fin—the tailfin dripping with chrome. The cars were designed, many of them, to suggest a racy look. The best were long and sleek with sharp, clean lines. The worst were heavily chromed, garishly colored, and had fins that were nothing but ugly.

They were, however, memorable for their performance, for the real joy and pleasure they gave their owners. How many kids grew up polishing the family

Below: Polishing the family car and dreaming of Saturday night.
Opposite top: The 1951 Ford Country Squire on the job.
Opposite bottom: Off on an autumn adventure with the 1953 Mercury Sport Coupe.

Ford
NORTHWEST

car and dreaming of Saturday night at the drive-in? How many hung around the local garage just to study what was under the hood? How many hours were spent arguing whether a Chevy would outrun a Buick in a drag race? That was the love affair. Those who remember still carry a torch for the cars of that time.

The cars of the 50s: ask anyone who remembers (and some who don't). These were the stuff of dreams, they'll tell you. How did these marvels of engineering and styling come about? Perhaps it all began with Henry Ford's Model T. The little black car with its affordable (no pun intended) price tag set free the great American wanderlust—the call of the open road. Suddenly, a whole new world beckoned and a generation of eager Americans joyously embraced mobility.

The little Model Ts went everywhere, from the Texas panhandle to the Great Smokies. They traveled the legendary Route 66. They traveled through Kansas dust storms. A utilitarian automobile, a workingman's vehicle—that was the Model T.

But there are always those who want more—more speed, more comfort, more style. Inventors, tinkerers, stylists, engineers—give any of them an idea and they'll improve upon it. So it was that in the 1920s the auto industry had begun to develop some of the great cars of all time. Such cars as the Duesenberg and the Cord set the public's pulses pounding and hearts dreaming. But such cars were only for the wealthy, driven by such people as the heroes of F Scott Fitzgerald's novels. The working man had to be content with something much less.

As the 1920s faded, the Great Depression hovered over the country. Unemployment and the breadlines became harsh realities. Families migrated from the somber dustbowls of Kansas and Oklahoma to California in search of a better life. They traveled the winding, unimproved roads, as always, in the faithful Model T, looking for work—any kind of work.

The Depression was a black time all across the nation. Banks in 38 states were closed. (Some would never

Above: The 1950 Pontiac Super Streak 8. Note the characteristic hood ornament.
Following page: A futuristic setting featuring a 1950 Olds 98 Futuramic.

open again.) Twelve million people were unemployed. Some sold apples on the street corners. Some picked cotton at 50 cents for 100 lbs. Many went into the Civilian Conservation Corps, the CCC as it was popularly known. Workers in the CCC made a dollar a day and their board. But it was also at this time, that Franklin Roosevelt, in an effort to unify the country and aid the economy, put forth a plan to improve and increase the network of highways across the country. This, of course, was going to affect the automobile industry. But, in the meantime, it gave thousands employment. Slowly, the nation's economy grew stronger.

Then on 7 December, 1941, the Japanese bombed Pearl Harbor. Within weeks, industry was mobilized for the war effort. Huge quotas went out for tanks, airplanes, and ships. Civilians put aside their dreams and went to work. Thousands of others went off to war.

It was a time of doing without. Americans, who had already experienced the hardships of the Depression, were undaunted by the wartime restrictions. They managed sugar rationing, shoe rationing, gasoline and tire rationing cheerfully, firm in the belief that each small sacrifice helped the fighting men toward winning.

School children saved scrap metal and bought savings stamps which would earn them defense bonds. Everyone planted victory gardens. Women went off to work in the factories, delighted to aid the defense effort and pleased for the income.

It was also a time when technology bloomed. Synthetic fibers, detergents, plastics, synthetic rubber all developed as wartime grew. Nylon was a new and exciting material. It had tremendous strength, but at the

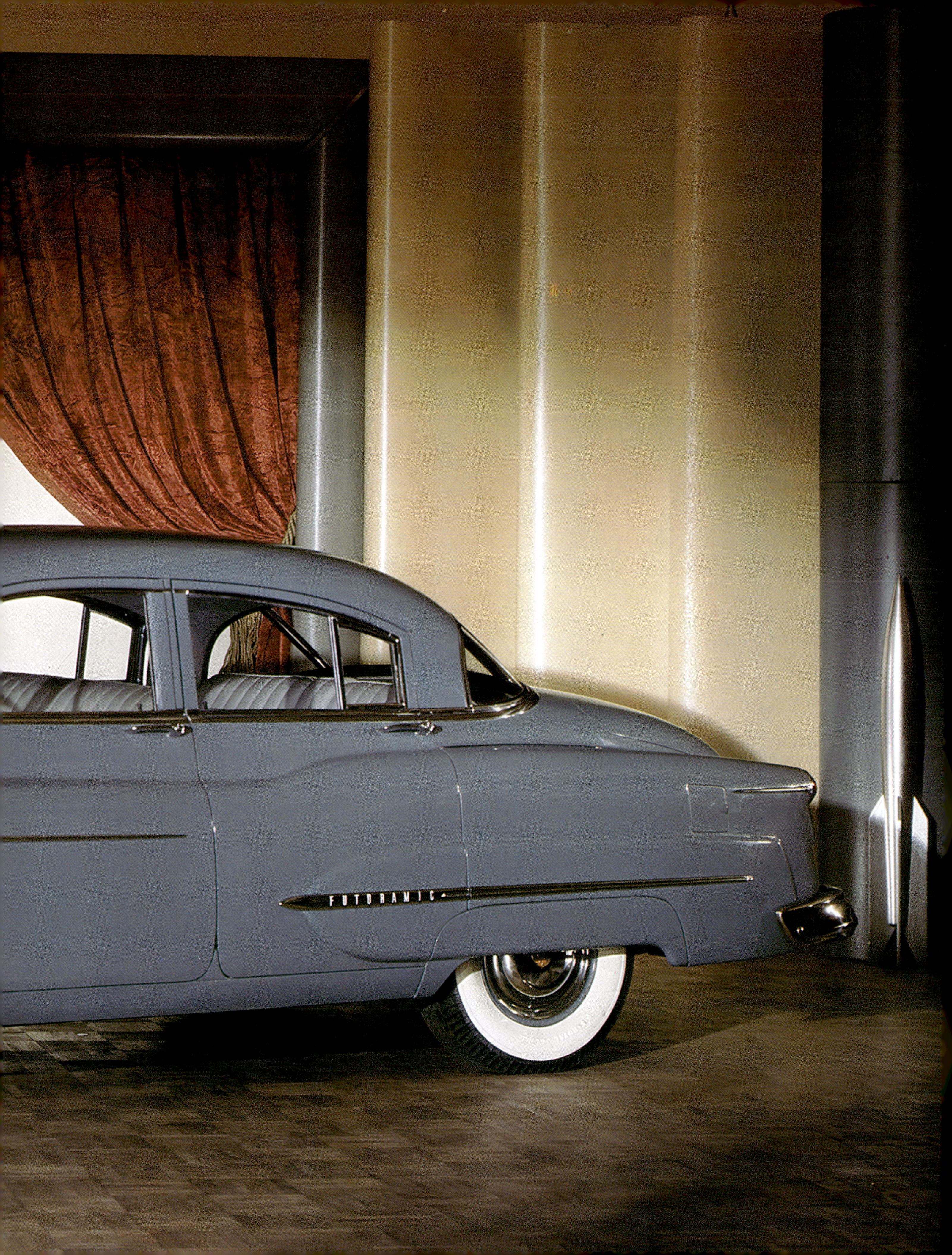
FUTURAMIC

same time was extremely light-weight. It was used primarily for parachutes. Rubber was in critical supply. Synthetic rubber proved stronger and more dependable.

By the time World War II was over, the nation was back on its feet. The privation of the Depression was gone. The War was over. Optimism was the spirit of the times. If you believed in happy endings, this was it, after two decades of gloom. Dwight D Eisenhower succeeded Harry Truman as President, and one of the great national projects during the Eisenhower era was the building of a network of interstate highways linking every state in the union. The project has been likened in its scope to the building of the pyramids. At the time, did anyone realize the effect this network of highways would have on the American life-style? No doubt, the automobile industry did.

Looking back, it's impossible not to see that the car of the 50s was a product of the times. The country was economically flush. A whole group of people who had come through hardship were ready for the good life as exemplified by a home in the suburbs and a new car.

A new car—the cars of the 50s were like nothing that ever came off the assembly line, before or since. They

Above: Dwight D Eisenhower. His administration did much to expand the interstate highway system.
Right: August H Wilhelm, a Mercury connoisseur, meets EM Boyson of Van Etta Motors, San Francisco, January 1954.

were the stuff of dreams. And the dream was possible for everyone! Glowing with chrome and colors Henry Ford never thought of, they drew fascinated crowds to the showrooms. People awaited breathlessly the model changeover, eager to see what the designers, stylists and engineers would come up with next.

The cars of the 50s did, indeed, reflect a kind of national exuberance. No one needed to settle for the utilitarian vehicle in this age of prosperity and optimism. However, there was more than just fins and chrome and planned obsolescence. Some of the most important automotive innovations were taking place at this time. One of the foremost was the automatic transmission, a real boon in city traffic. Critics said it lowered fuel economy, but in those times when gas was 25 cents a gallon, not too many people cared. The wraparound windshield was something new in the early 50s car. It added a certain amount of glamour, but also gave the driver a wider range of vision.

American drivers were power-mad in those days. A mild-mannered family man who got behind the wheel of the 54 Buick Century with its 195 horsepower V8 engine was suddenly transformed into a hot rod expert. Luxury and speed was what Americans wanted in their cars and it was what they got, at prices that would make today's car buyers drool! The 1956 Buick Century, for example, could go from 0 to 60 mph in 10 ½ seconds, exceed a speed of 110 mph, and cost about $3000.00.

Equally as important as speed and power was styling. No other period in automotive history has seen as much detail and concern with body shape, molding and trim. Some of the designs which came out of that period are looked on as classic—Studebaker's Loewy coupes were an example. These were designed, not by Raymond Loewy, but by Robert E Bourke who was chief of the Loewy Studios at South Bend. He had originally in-

Previous page: Country living with the genteel 1951 Lincoln.
Above: When gas was 25¢ a gallon and the attendant still washed your windows.
Opposite top: The sporty 1952 Lincoln Capri hardtop.
Opposite bottom: A sleek, white 1954 Desoto hardtop.

Century

Below: Buicks of the late 50s resorted to more and more chrome, as seen in this model 63 1958 Buick Century.

Bottom left: The ultimate in fins and chrome; a side view of the Buick Model 46R for 1958.

Bottom right: 1957 Buick Model 76R 2 door. The line had been completely restyled at a cost of several hundred million.

tended the design as a special show model until the Studebaker management saw it and bought the design. The clean, European styling is still considered one of the finest automotive designs of that era.

By contrast, one of the ugliest cars may have been the 1958 Buick with an enormous chrome grill and swooping chrome-decked tailfins. So awful is the design that it would probably serve as the archetypical overdone, overadorned 50s car.

But on the engineering front, innovation was in full flower. Chrysler evolved from an inefficient L-head engine to an exciting high performance car. The Chrysler Saratoga (a line dropped after 1952) with its hemi V8 engine and shorter (125.5) wheel base, was a frequent and often victorious contender at stock car races. Engineering, in this era, was Chrysler's strong point. The hemi became famous among stock car and drag racers. With modifications, it was possible to get as much as 1,000 hp from this efficient engine.

Along with the engineering, Chrysler evolved from the boxy look of the early 50s to the sleek designs of Virgil M Exner. Exner came to Chrysler from Studebaker. His taste ran toward classic European styling. Chrysler had already pioneered with the first hardtops shortly before the 1950s. But the car of those early years was plain and downright unexciting. Exner's cars were based on a Ghia bodied show car he'd first designed in 1951. Putting talent and innovation to work, he came up with the most attractive tailfins of the age. The 57 Chrysler 300-C was perhaps the best of the lot. The grill conservatively elegant, the fins clean and graceful, this was the car in which design and engineering reached a pinnacle. For though the 300-C was a big hairy-chested brute with enormous power, it was also safe and controllable—and beautiful.

Top: The 1954 Chrysler New Yorker wagon designed for the country gentleman.
Bottom: The 1954 Chrysler New Yorker Sedan—luxury and power!

Another good, old utilitarian car that received a major face-lifting in the 50s was the Chevrolet. Chevy, like Ford, had practically been a household word for automobile for some 50 years. Dependable, yes. Ordinary, yes. Staid, yes. Exciting, no. But came the 50s and things began to happen. There were still the ordinary family cars because there were still people that bought ordinary family cars. In addition, there was excitement embodied in the production of a lively little sports car called the Corvette. The Corvette first came out in 1953 as a fiberglass, two-seater which sold for $3500. Unlike its Chevy forebears which had operated with an engine known popularly as the 'stovebolt six', the Corvette sported a modified six cylinder engine which delivered

150 hp. Sports car fans, however, found it hard to reconcile themselves to the automatic transmission, despite increased hp.

Now, what to do about 'old utility?' It was clear, because of what was going on in the rest of the industry, that Chevy needed a better engine. So in 1953, the familiar 6 was revamped, with a higher compression ratio and a displacement of 235.5 cubic inches (3.8L) and up to 115 hp. (Compared with the 92 hp of the old 6 this was an improvement.) There it was—a steady, reliable engine. But it didn't exactly burn up the road. It took two engineers, Ed Cole and Harry Barr, to come up with something exciting. The two were always dreaming about how they'd design an engine. When the chance came in 1955, their design proved to be a milestone in automotive engines. With a displacement of 265 cubic inches, (4.4L) the new V8 weighed even less than the Chevy 6. Low reciprocating weight allowed higher rpm. Other innovations were die-cast heads with integral, interchangeable valve guides, aluminum slipper pistons, and a forged, pressed steel crankshaft. Cole and Barr had been so confident of their design that they had released the engine for tooling direct from the drawing boards—a multi-million dollar gamble! As it turned out, their confidence in the design was not misplaced. The engine turned out 162 hp at 4400 rpm or 180 hp at 4600 rpm with what Chevy called its POWER-PAK. The POWER-PAK was a four-barrel carburetor and dual exhausts which gave the engine its particular throaty roar—much admired by adolescent stock car racers.

Top: The Chevrolet Corvette, first American postwar sports car.
Bottom: Corvette; drivers loved its looks, hated the automatic transmission.
Following page: The 1953 Pontiac, traditional style on a larger scale.

FRDX

Facing page: The 1951 Ford Deluxe Sedan—higher and wider than a Chevy and very popular.
Top: The Chevy Nomad, one of the most attractive station wagons ever built.

Styling was the next consideration in the transformation of the once-dumpy car. Harley Earl was chief designer at Chevrolet at that time. His guideline was 'Go all the way and then back off.' Earl liked the egg-crate grill, part of the 1953 design; the public did not. Later versions featured broader, more conventional lines. Of the Earl design team, Carl Renner was responsible for the unusual hardtop station wagon, known as the Bel Air Nomad. It was probably the most beautiful station wagon ever designed. The first of the Nomads came out in 1955. But they were really impractical—two-door station wagons are inconvenient, as the public found.

It's sometimes interesting to know how automotive styles come about. In the early 50s, Ford cars were characterized by a distinctive grill called the 'spinner nose'. The design came in a roundabout way from Studebaker! Styling for the Ford had been open to many designers. One of those designers was Dick Caleal, whose friends, Robert Bourke and Holden Koto, were part of the Studebaker design team. Caleal requested design suggestions from his friends. Together the three built a quarter-scale clay model in the Caleal kitchen. To Mrs Caleal's dismay, they also baked it in her oven! The design was submitted to Ford's design chief, George Walker, and accepted with almost no changes as the Ford for 1949-50.

The Ford had always been a popular car and the early flat head V-8 engine was the delight of hot-rodders (and moonshiners) in the 50s. From 1951, Ford offered an optional two speed 'Ford-O-Matic' transmission. Before that, the company had tried, without success, to buy Studebaker's automatic shift.

The founder of the Ford Motor Company, the original Henry, would probably have done a swift rotation in his tomb, could he have seen the changes his little black car would undergo in the 50s. In the 1950-51 model year, Ford brought out the V-8 Crestliner. It was a very special edition, two-door vehicle, selling for a mere $1711. What made it special, however, was not its price tag, but its vivid two-tone color and padded vinyl top. The two-tone pinks and wild cerises would probably have turned Henry purple. He had been famous for a remark that people could have a Ford in any color they wanted 'so long as it's black.'

Ford's production climbed during the 50s. In 1954, the company introduced what was billed as the 'hottest engine in the low priced field.' This was an overhead valve, Y-block V-8 which could produce up to 130 hp. At the

Opposite top: The advertiser's dream for the young American family.
Opposite bottom: The 1955 Thunderbird—a classic success story.
Top: Essential to suburban living—the 1954 Ford Crestline Country Squire.
Bottom: The 1953 Ford Victoria Sedan, part of Ford's Golden Anniversary celebration.

same time, they introduced ball-joint front end suspension. These two innovations served to narrow the gap in engineering that existed between expensive and economy cars.

There were other innovations in styling: The Crestline Skyliner hardtop, developed by interior stylist L David Ash, had a front roof section made of transparent plastic.

Ford's exterior design during this period, 1954-55, was greatly influenced by Frank Hershey. There was a look of speed in the clean lines and highly chromed surfaces. It was also at this time that Ford's famous T-bird was born.

The Thunderbird, a spirited two-seater personal car, was the vision of General Manager Lewis D Crusoe. Wandering through a Paris auto show, he puzzled over the question of why Ford had never developed a sports model. The idea was handed to Frank Hershey and the first T-Bird came to the showrooms in 1955.

Another innovation from the Ford Motor Company was the Skyliner with the retractable hardtop. This came on the market in 1957. In the first year of production Ford sold 20,766 of these retractables, but production slowed quickly. The mechanism was complicated and expensive. The retractable roof cost $350 more than a standard convertible, which the public ultimately preferred.

Opposite: The 50s were the era of the convertible as evidenced by this 1951 Ford Custom.
Above: Symbols of the good life; a house in the country, a stable and a 1951 Ford Sedan.
Right: The 1953 Ford Mainliner, an ideal automobile for a shopping trip.

The times were a heyday for stylists, engineers and designers. Some of the engineers termed their work during this period as 'blue sky' projects, meaning that the sky was almost the limit on what might be accomplished. Some of the 'blue sky' projects turned out to be notable failures. Ford's Edsel was one of these.

Some of the most successful cars of the era became extinct by the late 50s and early 60s. But for a few brief years, the automobile was truly king, and a number of people prospered because of it. Advertisers played no small role in the rise of the 50s cars.

Chapter II. Cities, Suburbs and the Country Squire

'Our factory buildings and equipment, materials and processes are unapproached in the entire American automobile industry . . .' So began a magazine advertisement for the Columbia in 1906. Advertising in those years tended to be pompous and to reflect more on the manufacturer and the mechanics of the vehicle than on the buyer.

A great many changes had come to the automobile industry since this pre-World War I ad was written. The 50s saw the growth of the suburbs, the baby boom, leisure time, and prosperity. There was also the youth cult, the teenaged driver with more freedom and more money than teenagers had ever had before. There was a whole generation of Americans who had come through the hard times of the Great Depression and World War II. They felt it was time to 'live a little.' The advertising industry studied the market and wrote the script.

Below: The 1958 Chevy Bel Air Sport Sedan—longer, lower and slower. Race competition was on the wane.

Seventh heaven on wheels—

the Ford THUNDERBIRD

Wherever—whenever—your Thunderbird appears in public, the effect is electric. All eyes turn to its long, low, graceful beauty. All hearts say "That's for me!"

And if they only knew the full story!

If they could spend but half an hour in *your* seat. If they could listen to the dual-throated harmony of its tuned mufflers and twin exhausts. If they could feel the steepest hills melt before the might of the 198-h.p. Thunderbird Special V-8. If they could see the tachometer needle wind up, as the four-barrel carburetor and 8.5 to 1 compression ratio convert gasoline into road-ruling Trigger-Torque "Go!"

Then they'd sample a portion of your pride in *your* personal car. But you could show them more!

You could show them the way it takes the corners as if magnetized to the road. You could let them feel the lightning "take-off" with new Speed-Trigger Fordomatic Drive. You could show them how quickly the convertible top whisks into place—how easily the solid top lifts on and off—the all-steel body—the ample trunk space—the rich interiors—the telescoping steering wheel—the 4-way power seat. And should your Thunderbird have the optional power assists, they could note the convenience of power steering, power brakes and power window lifts.

You could show them this and more—how even routine driving becomes thrilling entertainment.

Yes, we're day-dreaming for you. But why not put yourself in the driver's seat and make this dream come true? The man to see is your Ford Dealer.

An exciting original by FORD

It was, of course, apparent that certain cars were built for certain markets. The young family in the suburbs was not going to consider a sports car as a family vehicle. And the station wagon was not exactly the car for the young single executive.

There were certain mottos and phrases which had grown up in the automobile advertising: *Ask The Man Who Owns One; When Better Cars are Built, Buick Will Build Them; There's a Ford in Your Future; We Aim to Take Care of Our Own.* These phrases were so intimately associated with the automobile that they were like part of the name.

Advertisers, creative people that they were, saw other possibilities that would sell more cars. People, they realized, no longer bought cars just for transportation. A car was a psychological machine. It said something about the person driving it. The svelte, spunky sports car was an example. Didn't it say that here was a very macho type of man with a love of speed, adventure and risk? More subtly, didn't it also imply that he was attractive, sexy, exciting, and just a little aloof? The advertisers loved this sort of thing. The public loved it even more!

Of course, the ad-men rightly realized that there were plenty of men, happily married with three kids, who still had quite a yen for speed and power. Detroit was building many powerful cars at this time, cars with the wind-

Opposite: Aptly described as seventh heaven, the 1955 T-Bird is still a heart-stealer today.

Top: Homeward bound traffic on a California freeway. Did they ever get there?

Above: Cars of the 50s were famed for their two-toned paint as well as chrome and fins.

Following page: A sample of the advertising of the times.

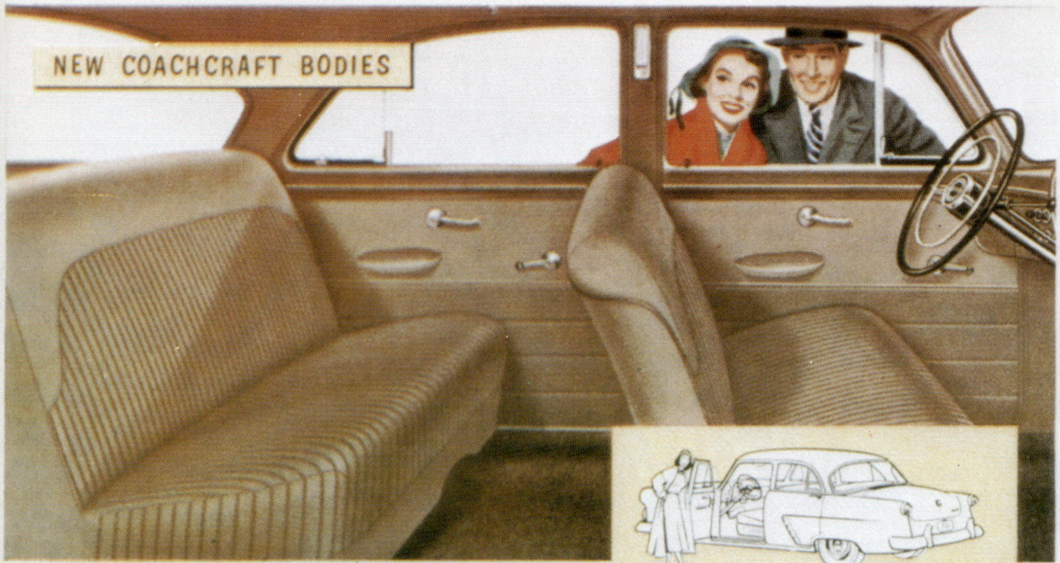

Styled to stay beautiful... Built to stay young The 1952 Ford has the newest, most advanced form of body construction. You get longer, stronger bodies, quality-built to the last detail. You get the most passenger comfort and convenience . . . the most baggage space . . . in the low-price field. You get distinctive interior trim . . . rich, long wearing upholstery fabrics, keyed to exterior colors and beautifully tailored in every detail. And because of new hull-tight construction you're shielded against water, dust and draft.

1. New contour-type seats with pillow-roll backs.
2. New counterbalanced hood and deck lid.
3. Automatic posture control front seat.
4. Narrower, stronger corner and center posts.
5. Roomiest luggage compartment in its field.
6. Girder-reinforced back window and windshield openings.
7. Weather-tight window and door seals.

The '52 Ford is designed to out-ride any car in its class New rear springs are longer. New rear shock absorbers are diagonally mounted. Front springs are tailored to the weight of each model. The wheelbase is longer . . . the front tread is wider . . . the center of gravity is lower. These and the many other features of Ford's Advanced Automatic Ride Control for 1952 level the roughest roads and take the tilt out of turns.

The ablest* car on the

The car that's made greater strides forward for '52 than any other in its class

Expect big things when you take the wheel of the '52 Ford! For here is the exciting, refreshing result of farsighted planning by the largest single engineering department in the industry! Here is a car unique not only in its price field but in the whole range of motoring! For no other car offers a choice of two power plants . . . Six or Eight . . . and each available with Fordomatic, Overdrive or Conventional transmission. No other offers so many body, color and upholstery combinations. A "Test Drive" will convince you that you can pay more—but you can't buy better than America's ablest car!

Meets the widest range of motorists' needs

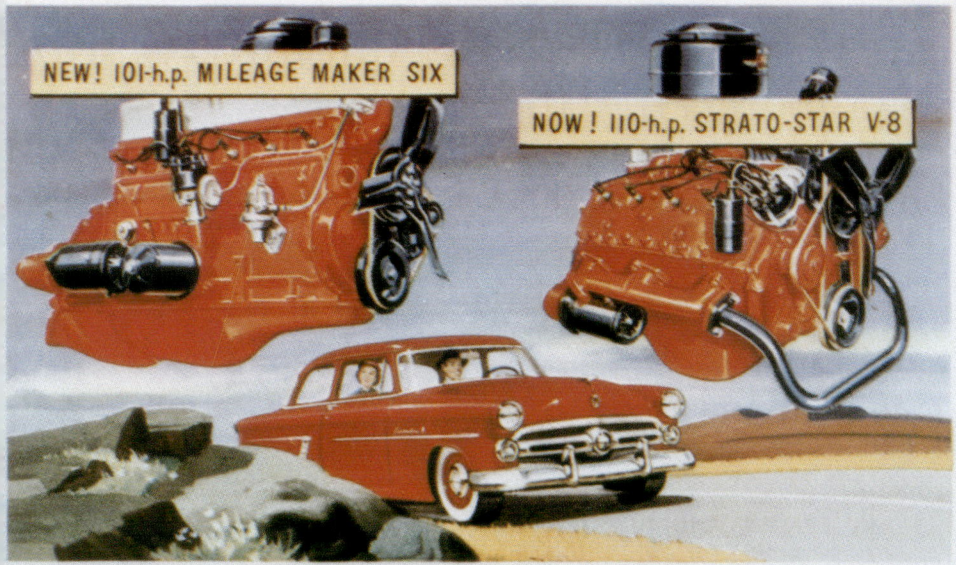

More power and more "go" per gallon. You get *both* in a '52 Ford, whether your choice is the all-new, high-compression 101-h.p. Mileage Maker Six, with free-turning overhead valves, or the famous Ford high-compression 110-h.p. Strato-Star V-8! Here are two performance-packed power plants that deliver their "go" on regular gas, thanks to Ford's exclusive Automatic Power Pilot. Both engines give you the quiet, long-wearing efficiency of super-fitted aluminum alloy pistons and new precision molded alloy crankshaft . . . exclusive to Ford in its field. Both give you the quick-starting advantage of Waterproof Ignition. In the entire "Six" field the Ford Mileage Maker engine, with its low-friction design, is the newest, finest and most modern! While the Ford Strato-Star V-8 is the most powerful engine . . . *and the only V-8* . . . in its class!

New Flight-Style Control Panel blends into the doors in a sweeping curve. Instruments are mounted so they're easier to read . . . and controls are placed where they're easier to reach.

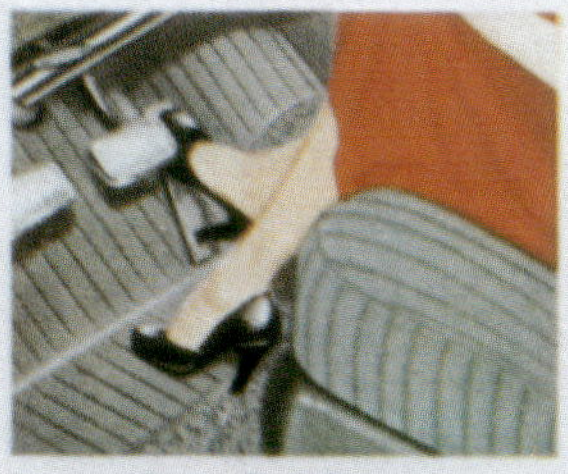

Power-Pivot Pedals are suspended from above, to operate with far less push! This method also eliminates dusty, drafty floor holes, gives you more foot room, and allows the brake master cylinder to be mounted under the hood for easier servicing.

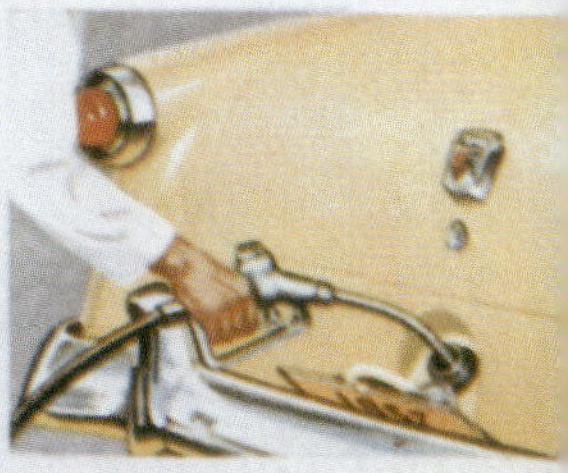

Center-Fill Fueling makes filling easier from either side of the car . . . license conceals filler cap. Center-Fill Fueling also does away with the long space-eating pipe in the trunk . . . another reason why Ford offers you more luggage space than any other low-priced car.

Does more things for more people at lower cost!

American Road! '52 Ford

Here's vision "unlimited" . . . front, sides and rear. You have the safety advantage of a big, one-piece curved windshield and a curved car-wide rear window.

White sidewall tires (if available) Fordomatic and Overdrive optional at extra cost. Equipment, accessories and trim subject to change without notice.

Below: The one-fifty series became the Delray in 1958 when Chevrolet revamped its line.

Following page: Status for a new leisure class—the 1957 Fairlane 500 convertible by Ford.

Dynaflow

The 1951 Buick Model 52; Buick at this time was one of the sleekest cars on the road. Note the portholes and the sweep-spear detailing of the side. Both became trademarks of Buick during the 50's.

Opposite top: The posh 1955 Ford Sunliner Convertible was part of the top-of-the line series for Ford and favored highly by the tennis set.
Opposite bottom: The 1956 Ford Country Squire took to good times like a duck takes to water.
Above: Team play on a football field; the 1952 Ford Customline could make going to the game a lot more fun.

swept look of speed, with tremendous horsepower. Here they were, smack in the face of the old double standard. What will you tell your wife when you go to test drive one of these riproarers? At this point, the ad-men played down the speed and power. Now they emphasized safety and handling ability. They pointed out luxurious upholstery, roominess and comfort. They hinted at the pleasure such a car would bring to routine chores like carpooling to Little League, downtown shopping, and trips to the dentist. They suggested Saturdays at antiques shows and auctions. Of course, people bought the car. And everyone was very happy.

Advertisers were well-tuned in to the American Dream. That dream included wealth, glamour, leisure, youth, and just plain getting away from the dull routine. Buick brought out a glorious convertible in 1951—the Le Sabre. An ad for this particular car shows it drawn up on a white sandy beach beneath swaying palm trees. The top is down (naturally) and sitting on the back of the seat is a suntanned dark-haired girl, attired appropriately in a bathing suit. Surely, an ad never covered all the bases quite so well or so completely. Women, who might have found the ad annoying, were also forced to think how delightful it would be to own such a car, to drive down the highway looking windblown, carefree, tanned and beautiful. To them the ad said, 'Buy this car and you'll be lovely.'

To the men, it said many other things. It was like a kind of Siren Song. The words sang of getting away to a private Shangri-La, of long days in the warm sun frolicking on the beach with the golden-skinned beauty. None of this was probably going to happen, but the car made it seem as though any moment it might. The sense of freedom, open air, sunlight and youth was all part of the convertible mystique. No matter that you were only driving to the corner grocery to pick up a quart of milk. The convertible made it seem you were bound on some exciting rendezvous. If only Walter Mitty had owned a convertible.

There were others whom the advertisers noticed. They had other dreams. The young, American family on the way up dreamed of a home in the country, four kids and a big dog—maybe even a stable! They needed a car for their kind of lifestyle. After all, there would be ballet lessons, gymnastics, swimming meets, the orthodontist, the pediatrician, summer camp, skating lessons, riding lessons. They needed a car—even two cars!

These were people who'd come through the austerity of the Depression. People who said, 'My child is going to have all the advantages I never had.'

The advertisers embroidered on the Dream. They pictured sleek station wagons drawn up in front of posh country clubs. Or they showed the kids and the family dog, cute as could be, piled into a roomy nine-passenger, about to embark for Grandma's. They showed wonderful, wood-sided station wagons parked outside elegant country estates. There was an aura here of landed gentry, private schools, and blueblood connections. And though for most people it wasn't true-to-life, still there was the element of possibility. For the station wagon also said things about the people who drove it.

A man behind the wheel of a station wagon was probably a family man who played golf on Saturdays, maybe went out hunting and fishing with a couple of good buddies, probably took his family camping in the summer. An ad for a 1959 Dodge Sierra station wagon shows three enthusiastic sportsmen heading out for bird hunting amid glorious fall foliage. One can almost feel the nip in the air! And what a lot of gear you could stow in that practical rear storage area.

Change the scene now and here are the ladies about to take the same wagon. They're the typical suburban matrons, beautifully groomed and nicely dressed. They would be off to a bridge luncheon, or to play tennis at the club. Or they might be bound to the city to visit the art galleries, do some shopping and meet their husbands for dinner. A station wagon was certainly a social vehicle, offering as it did, such a lot of room.

The 50s were the years of the 'Baby Boom.' The station wagon came into its own in these years. How else could you haul nine Little League players and all that equipment to the championship game? How else could you car pool six kids to nursery school? It was the only way to get Roxy and her litter to the vet's for their shots. Suburban mothers, who spent so much time on the road, cherished their 'wagons' almost as much as their favorite hairdressers. There were, as mentioned, the fun trips, too. You could pick up a bargain at a

Opposite: Air travel was becoming part of everyday living. What could be more convenient that the 1953 Ford Country Squire for transporting passengers and luggage to their destination?
Top: The station wagon gave rise to the all-American institution of the tailgate picnic, as the owners of this 1959 Desoto wagon could attest.

Bottom: Mercury had no fewer than six station wagon models for 1957. This one, the Colony Park, was one of the largest, being a nine-passenger four door model.
Following page: The station wagon was a boon to women everywhere as shown by this 1952 Ford Country Sedan.

Opposite top: The 1957 Ford Ranch Wagon was as practical for the rancher as for the executive in the city.
Opposite bottom: The 1954 Ford Skyliner, designed by L David Ash, was a forerunner of today's moonroofs. The unusual front roof section was made of transparent plastic. It was dropped in a year or two, however, since the plastic made the car too hot in summer.
Top: Glorious autumn weather lured people to put the top down and enjoy a last summertime fling. Note the styling of this 1957 Plymouth, revolutionary in a time of excess.
Bottom: Mainliner was the standard line for Ford in 1954. At that time due to a production war between Ford and GM, Fords were selling at below cost. GM was little hurt by this tactic but many independent car companies suffered.

FLOWERS
by Adelaide

The station wagon found favor with merchants as a delivery vehicle. While NASCAR mourned Chevy's loss of power, the 1958 Delray Sedan appealed to those who wanted lots of room and comfort.

The Ford Fairlane 500 featured an interesting option: a retractable hardtop roof. Developed originally for Continental, it was adopted for the Skyliner series.

Skyliner

The 1958 Chevrolet Impala was an extremely popular series in 1958 even though the line consisted of only two models—the hardtop and the convertible. They accounted for some 60,000 sales.

Following page: Plymouth for 1959 was number 3 among the top selling cars. Characterized by large fishy tailfins and an egg-crate grille, the 59 had a horsepower range of from 225 to 315.

The second of the two models in the Impala series was the Chevrolet Sport Coupe, a hardtop, show here as it looked in 1958.

Dodge Welcomes

Opposite top: A 1951 Dodge appearing in an advertisement of the times. Obviously an adman's idea of the perfect birthday present!
Opposite bottom left: The perfect setting to convey the sense of adventure driving the 1951 Dodge Hardtop would bring.
Opposite bottom: Exotic adventure or just driving home from the corner grocery? Either way, the 1951 Dodge could make it a pleasurable experience.
Top: The 1958 Chrysler New Yorker was considered a luxury car. Advertising helped to heighten the impression, as here.
Bottom: The 1957 Dodge Custom Royale was Dodge's luxury series, just right for the man who owned his own plane.

country auction and bring it home easily in the accommodating wagon. You could put all the skis on the roofrack and be off for the slopes in a jiffy. You could cart home a bushel of apples, two huge pumpkins and a gallon of cider from one of those quaint little country stands. And, best of all, the wonderful roominess of the wagon put distance between you and the kids and the dog! Ah, sweet oblivion!

The all-American automobile had evolved at this point into something more than just a vehicle. A lot of the appeal of certain models was as much psychological as anything else. Did anyone really need all that power, all that speed, all that chrome? Probably not. But it felt good and it looked good. Such sensuousness was irresistible to many. The Dodge was a case in point. In the early 50s, Dodge had been a very ho-hum automobile with the usual 6 cylinder engine and what was described as 'three-box' styling. In 1953, however, Dodge emerged as something far, far different from the stodgy car it had been.

As a division of Chrysler Corporation, Dodge fell heir to the hemi-head engine which Chrysler engineers had long been perfecting. The Dodge engine that year was a somewhat scaled down version of Chrysler's 331. Called the Red Ram V-8, the engine offered 140 hp plus. Further improved by Virgil Exner's styling, the Dodge took wings as a performance car. That year a Dodge V-8 won the Mobilgas Economy Run and broke nearly 200 records at the stock car races at Bonneville. Such records boosted the sales of Dodge enormously. One could point to the gasoline economy (Dodge V-8 got 23.4 mpg) and say what a good 'common sense' investment such a car was, but on the other hand, all that speed, power and grace didn't dampen enthusiasm, either. Behind the wheel of a Dodge, one could envision the long salt flats of Bonneville, the sting of alkali and the roar of the crowd.

A fantasy, yes but it lifted one out of the ordinary daily grind just to slip behind the wheel of such a car.

No one is immune to such fantasies. Nearly every car on the market was undergoing such a metamorphosis as Dodge. American tastes had grown more sophisticated and demanding. At the same time though, owning a car had become almost a necessity. Public transportation had declined or simply didn't exist. The trolleys and trains which had once been the major means of getting anywhere had curtailed their service or quietly died. Some large metropolitan areas kept their public transportation limping along, but for the most part it was simply easier to drive into the city than depend on the chancy bus schedules. The car was the link between home in the suburbs and the job in the city, the doctor's

office, the school, and down-town shopping. Because so much depended on getting to these places, Americans demanded reliability from their automobiles. Tailfins or no, nothing could be worse than being stuck in city traffic with an engine which just conked out—well, it could be worse if you had the kids and Rover.

This was a time, however, when automotive engineering had made tremendous strides. Not only were automobiles more powerful than they had ever been, they were extremely reliable. True, there were occasional 'lemons' but these were due more to production line flukes than to engineering defects. The manufacturers issued with each new car an owner's manual with specific maintenance instructions. This wasn't exactly a new idea, but with the newer engines it was a necessity. The owner's manual was required reading, listing oil changes, types of oil to use, tire rotation, times for engine tune-ups and the details to be checked at each tune-up. Toward the end of the 50s, some cars such as Chrysler developed a warranty against engine defects. Chrysler, whose motto was, 'we aim to take care of our own' was known for its outstanding engineering.

Chrysler owners were encouraged to take their cars back to the dealer for service and parts rather than going to the local gas station. This kind of service earned consumer loyalty, kept people coming into the showroom 'just to look' at newer models and also increased business for the dealer. Most car dealers had picked up on the service angle. It was a very logical outgrowth of sales. If you sold it, why not service it? It was also part of the reliability factor. A local mechanic who saw a car on a regular basis got to 'know' it and its owner very well. The busy suburban family relied on the mechanic for their car problems as much as they relied on their pediatrician for the children's ills. Service became a consideration in the sale of a car.

That the American Lifestyle was changing sharply in this decade was apparent. That the automobile had influenced this change was also apparent. The burgeoning middle class, the new prosperity, the network of fine highways that spread across the country and, in no small way, the Great American Dream, had changed the country more dramatically than anyone would ever have guessed.

Opposite: The 1954 Dodge found just as much favor with the folks down home as well as with the city cousins.
Above: Conservative styling accounted for Plymouth's lack of popularity in 1954.

Chapter III. Power Steering, Automatic Transmissions and the Women

Above: The 1955 Oldsmobile Holiday in two-toned style. Milady's dress is called a sheath, for obvious reasons.
Opposite top: A summer holiday in a 1954 Mercury Monterey convertible.
Opposite bottom: Detail of the steering wheel and dash of the 1953 Packard Patrician.

The American Lifestyle had changed. In the 30s and 40s, the city had been the place to live. There was the convenience of public transportation, neighborhood shopping, and the close proximity of theaters, galleries and museums. Cities in those years seemed to offer all the advantages of the good life. But Americans of the 50s yearned for space, fresh air, wholesome country living and the small towns that spoke of an easier, slower way of life. The country or a small town, that was the place to raise children. Many cities were falling to slow decay. They were dirty, they were crowded, the neighborhoods had changed, crime was growing and there simply wasn't enough good housing.

There was also a tremendous building boom going on. Young veterans of both World War II and the Korean Conflict needed homes for their families. Suburban houses sprouted like mushrooms. Row on row on row of neat little look-alike homes sprang up on streets called Shady Lane (no trees, of course), or Wendy's Way. They looked very barren, but that didn't matter. They also looked so much alike that people made jokes about walking into the wrong house, and that they were all produced by a giant cookie cutter. What made them very strange, however, was the lack of the usual village center with its shops, churches, schools and hospitals.

In their exodus to the country, the families of the 50s had left behind all the services the cities provided. It was no longer an easy two-block walk to the grocery store but a real 15-mile pilgrimage twice a week. And it was a five-mile run to the nearest school. Luckily there were a lot of children, so carpools could be arranged. The car was in daily use. And it was Mom who chauffeured. A lot of things happened because of this subur-

Below: The 1954 Cadillac Series 62. Long known for luxury and elegance, Cadillac of the 50s had an engine renowned for efficiency and performance.
Following page: An ideal car to get away from it all, the Plymouth Fury for 1959 was well-known for its high performance engine.

Fury

Below: Off to the polo club in the 1953 Series 62 Cadillac. The top is down, of course, to allow its owners to soak up the glorious California sun!

Below: The Dodge Custom Royale in emerald green, the girl in mink, both sure to turn heads in 1958.

Custom Royal

ban growth. Traffic swelled. Roads improved. And cars became easier and safer to drive.

The automatic transmission appeared in the late forties. Consumers eyed it cautiously. Sports-car types who preferred 'four on the floor' openly sneered and continued to shift for themselves. But Mom loved it. Driving as she did, in all kinds of traffic, the automatic shift was a joy. None of the constant high to low to second, with the automatic shift, one could pay more attention to traffic and to finding a place to park!

That was another problem, finding a place to park. One had to drive into the city to shop, along with a million other people. Traffic was horrible, parking was impossible and the whole ordeal threatened your sanity. But then, on cue, came a wonderful invention. Far from the madding crowd, with acres of parking space and lots and lots of shops came the shopping mall. It was a godsend to the suburban dweller. You still had to drive to the mall but there was less traffic and always a parking spot.

Americans at this time were developing a taste for luxury. The house on Wendy's Way had wall-to-wall carpets and the new den had floor-to-ceiling oak paneling. There was also a downstairs powder room. How did anyone manage with just one bathroom? And there was a 'rec' room in the basement with TV and a bar and a stereophonic phonograph. In the beginning it was fun, but then luxuries became necessities. No one thought twice about building a house with 2½ baths and wall-to-wall carpeting was *de rigueur*.

The taste of luxury was reflected just as much in the family car. Carpeting and upholstery were just as elegant as in the living room at home. There were numerous small conveniences in the new automobiles. Many were standard equipment. Others were optional. There were cigar lighters, tinted glass, map lights, arm rests, bucket seats and air conditioners. Packard did away

Above: Resorts flourished in the 50s and the best way to be seen was in the 1952 Cadillac Series 62 Convertible.
Opposite top: The streets of San Francisco: the scene is the top of Nob Hill around the mid 50's. Coming toward us is a Cadillac with the familiar bumper bullets.
Opposite below: The Chrysler of 1953 showing the dowdy three box styling of that year.

with the cluttered 'glove compartment' and offered a drawer instead. It was highly practical but no other car ever adopted the idea. Air conditioning was a real boon to the motorist. It offered a cool pleasant ride on the hottest day. It also offered peace from traffic noise, since the windows had to be rolled up when the unit was operating. And bucket seats found a ready market in the tall man—short lady combination. That meant that Mom could drive Dad to the station without his having to sit with his knees up by his ears!

The luxury car of luxury cars has always been the Cadillac. So it was in the 50s and so it will probably always be. The Cadillac of the early 50s was one of the best road cars of that time. They were expensive and justifiably so with their custom interiors and panoramic windshields. Long known as the 'Standard of the World', the Cadillac of the 50s was an elegant car. The Cadillac Eldorado was a limited edition in 1953. Five hundred thirty-two were built that year. They were priced at $7750 which made them the most expensive car of that year. The Eldorado convertible was one of the most beautiful cars ever. A special metal boot covered the folded-down convertible top. The interior styling, all of it custom, was exquisite. It was indeed a classic.

In 1957, Cadillac brought out the Eldorado Brougham, a very expensive ($13,000) and a very unusual car. The Brougham featured a brushed aluminum roof, quadruple head lights and the distinctive Harley Earl styling. The Brougham was a pillarless sedan. Looking like a very regal 'Hard Top' with doors that opened in the center, it was also equipped with air suspension. Air suspension had been around since 1952, but it had never been used on a passenger car before. It provided, or was supposed to provide, a very smooth, level ride. But because the cost and maintenance of air suspension was so high, Cadillac soon dropped this system.

Chrysler was another of the luxury cars of the 1950s. It was not quite in the same class as the Cadillac, but still a fine car known for excellent engineering and handling ease. In 1953, Chrysler had introduced a two-speed automatic transmission known as PowerFlite. PowerFlite had evolved into a 3-speed transmission called TorqueFlite by 1957. TorqueFlite was one of the finest

Below: An old stone fence, a sunny spring day, a lovely drive in a 1951 Cadillac Sedan.

Following page: The summer of 1957; a sidewalk cafe and a Cadillac Convertible—the stuff of dreams!

AV-7553

Opposite top: The 50s were a time to experiment. Not only styles in automobiles but also colors underwent dramatic changes as witness this 1956 Lincoln Premiere, which was painted pink!
Opposite bottom: 1957 was the first major body change for Lincoln since 1951. Pointed tailfins showed that even the elegant Lincoln was influenced by trends.

Top: The Chrysler New Yorker for 1959; soaring tailfins pleased the public and the new wedge-head engine excited curiosity.
Bottom: The Dodge Royal Lancer. Pink seems hardly the color but it doubtless was the lady's choice.

Opposite: The 1955 Cadillac Eldorado Seville, stylish anywhere but especially in the French Quarter of New Orleans.
Top: The 1956 Cadillac 60 Special Sedan, showing the slow evolution of the traditional design. The Cadillac of the late 50s lacked the clean styling of the earlier models.

Bottom: 1958 Cadillac Eldorado Brougham; the sharp tailfins over the taillights were a trademark of the Eldorado Series.
Following page: The 1955 Lincoln, or how to feel like a celebrity. The styling was especially conservative, and therefore outstanding.

Ed Sullivan, M.C. of Toast of the Town, and Julia Meade introduce New Lincoln. Control room monitor sets show new Turbo-Drive lever, new rear deck, new longer body, new front assembly

Camera one! Close up! Take the

And don't miss Lincoln's new, smoother and faster Turbo-Drive; new wide-range high torque V-8 engine!

ED SULLIVAN and Julia Meade are waiting. Then—the show's on. And, sparkling in homes across the nation is the new, incomparably finer Lincoln for 1955.

It's sheer pleasure to look at the new longer sweeping lines of the body. You'll like to linger over the colorful beauty so unusual among fine cars. You'll want to live in the distinctive interiors, richer in quality, in exquisite details, than any other car in the fine car field.

But perhaps more exciting is the story on performance. *Lincoln* performance that clinched the first *two* places (for the third year in a row) in the large stock car division of the Pan-American Road Race in Mexico. Performance that defeated all other major American fine cars in the most grueling test of them all.

In these new 1955 models, you'll see Lincoln performance further enhanced by new Turbo-Drive—the transmission that has been called the biggest news in automatic drives since the first one 15 years ago. Here is no frustrating lag, no unpleasant jerk from one gear to the next. With Lincoln's Turbo-Drive you enjoy one unbroken sweep

Lincoln's new high torque V-8 engine.

ew Lincoln for 1955

smooth, silent power, from start to superhighway speed limits. Here too is a perfect marriage of the newest development in automatic transmissions with the newest type of V-8 engine. You'll feel difference, particularly in the normal speeds where you do most your driving. You'll enjoy instant power—when you need it and ere you need it. For this is the finest power plant ever made by the rld's foremost builders of V-8 engines. Your Lincoln dealer invites to drive a Lincoln or Lincoln Capri. You'll know you've made a nderful discovery the moment that Lincoln's wheels begin to turn!

NEW 1955

LINCOLN

for modern living

Above: The ultimate luxury; the 1958 Cadillac Series 75 Limousine. Is madam bound for Tiffany's or Bloomingdale's?

Following page: The 1958 Crown Imperial Limousine inherited its elegance by way of Italy where the line had been built by Ghia of Turin. The basic kit was shipped to Torino where Italian craftsmen spent a month building each car. Suggested retail price? $15,075!

automatic transmissions ever built. Chrysler also developed the Torsion-Aire ride. This consisted of torsion bars on the front wheels to eliminate road shock. Torsion bars were a major contribution to easy handling.

Lincoln had always been known as a luxurious but sedate automobile. In the 50s, it began a slow transformation. The first new development was the V-8 valve-in-head engine capable of 160 hp when first introduced in 1952. It boasted such innovations as oversized intake valves which allowed for greater efficiency and output per cubic inch of engine size. There were eight counterweights on the crankshaft instead of the usual six, making it one of the smoothest engines ever. By the time the 1953 models were coming out, the engine could produce 205 hp with greater efficiency than either Cadillac or Chrysler.

Starting in 1952 Lincolns were also equipped with ball-joint front suspension. The ball-joint suspension proved to be a very controllable, flexible system. Further improvements were recirculating-ball power steering, sound-deadening insulation and oversized drum brakes, plus an optional four-way power seat. There was also optional factory air conditioning with flow-through ventilation. The interior, with its fine quality fabric and leathers, reflected the ultimate in quiet good taste.

Kaiser was an interesting luxury car. The 1951 model prompted a good deal of enthusiasm. It offered more glass, ease of handling and some of the most unique styling of the 50s. Most luxurious of all was the 1953 Kaiser hardtop Dragon sedan. The Dragon sported gold-plated exterior trim plus a padded top. Inside, the car was upholstered in a fabric called 'Laguna' cloth created by fashion designer Marie Nichols. The Dragon had everything; tinted glass, Hydra-Matic drive, whitewall tires, dual-speaker radio and a special custom carpeting on the floor and trunk. There was a gold medallion on the dash which could be engraved with the owner's name. All of these were standard accoutrements on the Dragon. But such a spectacular car demanded an equally spectacular price. The Dragon's $3320 tag did not make it especially popular with the public. Only 1277 Dragons were ever built.

Above: A 1959 Cadillac Coupe deVille; Cadillac joined the trend to tail fins as well as some quite garish chrome trim.

The Imperial, an outgrowth of Chrysler's top line, became a separate make of automobile in 1955. It was totally a luxury car with the same sort of quiet taste seen in Cadillac and Lincoln. The Imperial was powered by a 331 cubic-inch (5.4L) V-8 engine, the familiar 'hemi' which produced 250 hp. In 1956, the new models featured a bored-out version of the same engine—354 cubic inches (5.8L) and capable of 280 hp. PowerFlite transmission on the Imperial was standard. The only special option was air conditioning. By 1957, the Imperial had evolved the huge tailfins so typical of Virgil Exner's Forward look. These came standard with the TorqueFlite three-speed transmission and a formidable 392 hemi-head engine which produced 325 hp. It was arresting, it was exciting and it outsold Lincoln for the first time ever. Dealers were consistently frustrated by people who still referred to the car as the Chrysler Imperial. Chrysler, while a fine car, never carried the prestige that Cadillac (Imperial's rival) did.

Packard was an old name in luxury cars. Before the Great Depression, Packard had been famous for its tasteful and expensive automobiles. But the company would have died in the 30s had it not brought out a line of lower priced cars. When the automobile companies began building again in 1945, Packard offered its basic prewar design again (as did nearly all the auto manufacturers). The style was ugly and ungainly, known by many as the 'pregnant elephant' which was, unfortunately, an apt description of the car.

Style, however, did not interfere with the roadability of the Packard. The Packard was beautifully engineered, smooth and powerful on the road. The 'pregnant elephant' was totally re-designed for 1951 by John Reinhart. Packard, unfortunately, clung to its lower-priced line while at the same time it brought out the more traditional Packard. Among these more traditional types was the Mayfair which came out in both a

hardtop and a convertible. The Mayfair was elegantly trimmed, a lively, sporty car which appealed to buyers.

Packard was limping along when James Nance became president of the Company in 1952. The plant was working at 50 percent of capacity when he took over. Nance relegated the inexpensive line to a separate make called the Clipper and Packard went back to building luxury cars. Patrician was the top of the Packard line, a formal car with a leather top and tiny rear windows, priced at $6531 in 1953. In the same year, Packard introduced a glamorous convertible called the Caribbean as a limited edition. The Caribbean, with its 180 hp engine, was well received and outsold Cadillac's Eldorado that year.

Hudson in the 50s was a marginal luxury car. It was a large unit-body automobile which one stepped down into, a car which seemed to place more emphasis on comfort than style. The Hudson Hornet won fame as a spunky contender in the NASCAR races. The Jet Liner series, Hudson's luxury line, sparked a sort of American-Italian marriage which culminated in the exciting looking Italia. The Italia was a four-passenger *gran turismo* designed by Frank Spring, Hudson's chief designer and built by Carrozzeria Touring Co, of Milan. The Italia was all that the dowdy Hudson was not. It had elegance and styling, wraparound windshields, doors which were out into the roofline, functional airscoops, leather seats, and flow-through ventilation. But Hudson's finances were shaky. There was not enough money for a firm commitment to this car so only 25 plus the prototype and a single four-door model called the X-161 were ever produced. They were sold at $4800 each. They were Hudson's last attempt at a luxury car. In 1955 Hudson and Nash merged and Hudson faded.

The American family, as part of its taste for luxury, now often owned two cars. Two cars, in fact, were often a necessity. Dad, who commuted to work in the city, needed a car to get him at least as far as the Park and Ride lot. Mom, at home with all the burgeoning family responsibilities, also relied on the car to handle the myriad errands which she faced. For a while, they managed nicely with one car. Mom merely scheduled all the errands for one particular day. On that day she drove Dad to the station and the car was hers. But there were numerous times when two cars would ease the conflict, so they succumbed and bought a station wagon which became Mom's car and a regular sedan which Dad used to drive to work.

No one thought much about the inefficiencies of such a situation. Driving a full-sized car with a powerful en-

gine in city traffic or leaving it parked in a parking lot all day was what everyone did. There was really not much choice in the matter, because no one had thought of a commuter car.

No one, that is, except George Mason of Nash. Contrary to every other manufacturer of the times, George Mason loved little cars. The Nash Rambler was his 'baby', so to speak. The Big Three auto manufacturers had all given up on the compact car. But George Mason, with great foresight, saw the value of the small car, particularly since none of the other companies had such a model. Rambler came out in the early 50s as a two-door station wagon and an unusual landau convertible. The convertible, unlike any other, had permanently fixed window frames. Only the roof folded down. In 1951, a hardtop was added to the line. But the top seller for Rambler was the practical and attractive wagon. It was an ideal suburban car, in fact 22 percent of the wagons sold at that time were Ramblers. For a small automobile company, that was highly successful.

It hardly needs to be mentioned that more and more women drove. Time was when driving had been the prerogative of the man of the house. But by the 50s, the women had taken over the wheel, and they loved it. Car manufacturers were beginning to realize what dealers had known all long, that an automobile had to appeal to the wife as well as the husband. Dodge went so far as to manufacture a show car called La Femme, a Custom Royal Lancer two-door hardtop. It featured a pink exterior and white upholstery. Other little custom accoutrements were a folding umbrella and a handbag designed to rest in the backs of the front seats. The pink and white car caused a real stir at automotive shows in 1955 and 56. The interest seemed strong enough to send the car into serious production, but luckily Dodge thought better of it. Only a few of these cars were ever produced.

For the American woman, the car was one of the great liberating forces of her life. It gave her the freedom and the ability to travel anywhere she pleased with ease and comfort that had never existed before. There was security in the big, powerful, reliable cars and there was real pleasure and exhilaration in driving them.

Above: The 1957 Imperial managed to beat out its arch-rival Lincoln in sales that year. 38,000 of the luxury cars were sold, a banner year indeed.
Following spread left: An advertisement for Hudson. 1951 marked the introduction of the Hornet, a car which made a name for itself in NASCAR history.
Following spread right: Advertisement for the Nash Airflite.

Famous "step-down" design steps out !

Hudson for '51

presents 4 rugged series
adds spectacular new car
scores engine sensation
introduces Skyliner Styling

PRICES BEGIN
JUST ABOVE THE LOWEST

Starring the fabulous new

Tune in THE BILLY ROSE SHOW • ABC-TV Network

HUDSON HORNET

and its sensational new H-145 ENGINE

PLUS HYDRA-MATIC DRIVE*

Hudson's here for '51—with four rugged series of matchless new cars! The lower-priced **Pacemaker Custom.** The renowned **Super-Six Custom.** The luxurious **Commodore Custom.** And the fabulous **Hudson Hornet!**

Yes, there's a spectacular addition to Hudson's great line-up of new cars—the Hudson Hornet . . .

A magnificent newcomer—powered by the amazing, new H-145 engine, which delivers sensational high-compression performance—and does it on regular gasoline!

But no matter which Hudson you choose, you get outstanding performance, plus gorgeous new Skyliner Styling! Custom-luxury interiors! Clean-lined, low-built beauty outside! Massive front-end design! A definite look of the future all around!

It's the auto show of the year! New Hudsons for '51—at your nearby dealer's now! Won't you accept our invitation, see them soon?

**Optional at extra cost on Hudson Hornet Series and Commodore Custom Series*

Miracle H-Power is here! It's the world's most thrilling high-compression performance! With the sensational, new H-145 engine in the distinguished new Hudson Hornet, there's blazing getaway—entirely new command of the road at any speed—from an engine that is marvelously smooth in action—an engine superbly simple in design for lowest upkeep costs! And—you get the peak of this high-compression performance with regular gasoline!

Nash Presents America's Newest Hardtop Convertible

The Rambler "Country Club"

SEE SOMETHING ENTIRELY NEW in automobiles—the Nash Rambler in a dazzling new hardtop convertible. Distinctively new in custom luxury—with new line-of-sight visibility—and *priced with the lowest!* It rides like a dream—romps up the hills with light-footed sureness—handles with an ease you never felt before—and gets up to 30 miles a gallon at average highway speed. Think of having this smart beauty with radio, Weather Eye Conditioned Air System, Directional signals—nearly $300 worth of custom "extras"—*at no extra cost.*

Come see and drive this newest Rambler Airflyte, dashing companion car to the distinguished Ambassador and popular Statesman. See your nearby Nash dealer and get the best car for the years ahead.

Before You Decide, Take an Airflyte Ride—in the World's Most Modern Car

Nash Airflyte

THE AMBASSADOR
THE STATESMAN
THE RAMBLER

Nash Motors
Division of Nash-Kelvinator Corp.
Detroit 32, Mich.

That Continental Flair! The open-air fun of a convertible with solid steel above—with over 17 feet of clear glass around you! Completely custom with foam-sponge cushions upholstered in needle-point.

World's Safest Convertible is also the most economical car! Smashing all records for miles to the gallon in the 1951 Mobilgas Economy Run, the dashing Rambler All-Weather Convertible averaged 31.05 m.p.g.

Two Cars In One—The Rambler All-Purpose Sedan is America's most practical car. A luxuriously-appointed family sedan, it converts into a spacious station wagon—with a 6 foot platform—at the drop of a seat!

See Them All! In addition to the thrilling new Nash Rambler Country Club, see the other Airflytes—the Rambler Station Wagon or Greenbrier All-Purpose Sedans . . . the popular Statesman . . . and the distinguished Ambassador. All are America's most modern cars . . . built the *better* way—with Airflyte Construction.

FOR TV FUN! Watch Paul Whiteman TV TEEN CLUB on ABC, presented by your Nash and Kelvinator dealers. See your paper for time.

Opposite: Detail of the taillight from a 1959 Cadillac Fleetwood.
Top: The 1956 Imperial was based on a design by Virgil Exner and on the Chrysler K-310 sports car. Today they are considered desirable collector's cars.

Following page: Detail of a 1955 Imperial taillight. These were known as bomb taillights and were one of the identifying marks of the Imperial.
Bottom: An ad for the Packard Clipper of 1954. Clipper had not yet become a separate line.

Here's America's New

The New Packard

Here's your opportunity to own at only a few hundred dollars more than

Announcement of the beautiful new *Packard* CLIPPER was bound to make news. And it did!

People who love the sturdiness and elbowroom of a truly big car—but don't quite feel they can afford one—are looking at this big new *Packard* CLIPPER, riding in it, and ordering it!

In all truth, the new *Packard* CLIPPER is enjoying public response—far beyond expectations—and has, since the first day it was shown!

That's because the value is there, and the price is right. So right.

How can Packard do it? Deliver so much big-car value and performance at medium-car prices?

FIRST: It's Packard engineering—traditionally fine, historically dependable. Packard, you remember, is the oldest maker of fine quality cars in America.

SECOND: Packard occupies a unique manufacturing position, for Packard alone with 54 years' experience in fine car building,

Medium-Priced Car!

160-horsepower Packard Deluxe Clipper. Be sure to see and drive it.

CLIPPER

and drive a really fine automobile you'd pay for a car in the lowest-priced field!

combines craftsmanship of the highest character, and modern mass production techniques, to produce greater values.

In addition to greater values, you get Packard's contour styling that is setting the new trend in automotive design. Contour styling means not only a handsomer car, but better visibility. You get the smoothness and comfort of the famous Packard ride, too—*real big-car ride!*

You get the unforgettable kitten-smooth, whip-quick pull and zoom of the Packard Thunderbolt-8 Engine—*real big-car power!*

In all, you get more than 70 big-car features that Packard has built into the medium-priced CLIPPER!

If you plan to buy a car in the $2,500 price-class be sure to see and drive the new *Packard* CLIPPER. Compare it with other medium-priced cars. Surprisingly enough the CLIPPER costs only a few hundred dollars more than the cars in the lowest-priced field. And, of course, there's a wide range of beautiful new CLIPPER models, any one of which will give you a *lift*, as well as a ride, anytime you drive it!

New Packard
CLIPPER

In addition to the Clipper, PACKARD is building today a car so beautiful and fine that it is applauded everywhere as "America's new choice in fine cars." Ask the man who owns one—today!

Chapter IV.
White Bucks and Saddleshoes

Two things did more to put American teenagers on wheels in the 50s than anything else. One was the ready availability of jobs in those years and the other was the auto manufacturer's policy of 'planned obsolescence.'

Teenagers of the 50s, for the first time in history, had money to spend, more money than any teenage generation before. Like their elders, they were intrigued with cars. They spent their Saturdays and their free time looking at cars, working on cars, talking cars, going to and participating in 'drag races'. Owning a car then, as now, was a special badge of maturity and freedom. And if you owned the 'right' car, you would have to beat the girls (or boys) off with a stick!

Planned obsolescence was a kind of scheme that worked because the automobile companies were riding the tide of a seller's market. Nearly every year, when the new models came out, there would be changes in the cars. Every two to three years there would be a dramatic styling change. And yearly, there would be engineering changes. Sometimes there would be only minor engine innovations. But even so, last year's car was just not as up-to-date or glamorous as the newest model. So, many people changed cars every two or three years. The old models were far from worn out. Many, in fact, were just nicely broken in. And this was where the teenage market came in. For a little money, one could go down to Easy Harry's Used Car Lot and make himself a heck of a deal on a '54 Dodge or a '53 Chevy. 'A beautiful car,' Harry would say, 'not a scratch on it, purrs like a kitten. Sure, try it out.'

The funny thing was that this car was all that Harry said it was. Of course, with a little work it would blow everybody away at the dragstrip! That was part of the fun in owning a car—just seeing how much power you might get from that engine by varying the bore and stroke.

Below: Another view of the 1955 Pontiac. The car had been completely revised for the model year 1955 and boasted 109 new features, including a V-8 engine. *Opposite:* A 1955 Pontiac sporting the traditional dice hanging from the rear view mirror.

BZB 803
CLUB INTL

Above: For 1955, Chevrolet introduced a revolutionary V-8 engine; the design of engineers Ed Cole and Harry Barr became the basis for all future Chevy engines. *Opposite:* The Chevrolet of 1954 still retained much of styling of earlier 50's cars.

The Ford flat-head V-8 was a prime target for the hot-rodder. With a little tinkering and a few modifications, the V-8 could churn out 110 hp at 3800 rpm.

Chrysler Corporation, with its much coveted hemi-head engine, became one of the all-time delights of the hot-rod crowd. The engine, with minor modifications to exhaust, carburetors, and camshaft, might achieve 352 hp. Drag racers who really worked on the engine could get as much as 1,000 hp from the hemi. But such work was costly and complicated. To begin with, the hemi-with its interchangeable heads, was heavy and expensive. Modifying it required double rocker shafts, push-rods, rockers and other expensive goodies. It took time and money to achieve all the power the hemi was capable of delivering. A lot of kids had to be satisfied with the dream, but even that was enough. Parents and the local police tended to view such vehicles with a very critical eye.

When Chevrolet came out with its V-8 in 1955, it also became another car to delight the teenagers. The light-weight 265 could deliver 162 hp at 4400 rpm. Its low reciprocating weight helped to boost the rpm. It was a great car for the drag-strip.

The real dream cars of those years, however, were Ford's snazzy Thunderbird (the two-seater model) and Chevy's Corvette. Anyone who was lucky, a born salesman, or possessed of an innocent parent might con his family into buying such a car 'for commuting'. The next thing was to con the parents into letting you drive it! Should you, by some strange quirk of fate, accomplish these various tasks, then the world was yours, The Prom Queen ignored the football hero, every girl in the senior class was panting to go out with you and your buddies all wanted to look under the hood. There was no greater victory than to pull into the local root beer

stand on a Saturday night in such a super car with two or three of the most desirable cheerleaders in tow. Ah, how sweet it was! That is, it was sweet until you were awakened the next morning by an irate father who asked why you hadn't thought to refill the gas tank.

The 'T-Bird' first came out in 1955. With its rakish looks, it became an immediate success—even a legend. Ford's overhead-valve Y-block V-8 had been bored out to 292 cubic inches (4.9L) for the Bird. The engine was thus capable of producing nearly 200 hp. The first 1955 edition sold over 16,000 copies. Rock stars sang about it, dealers praised it, and fathers fumed every time the kids took it out.

Chevy's Corvette had been introduced to the public in 1953. It was America's first postwar sports car. Like the T-Bird, it was a two-seater, ideally cozy with the right person! Style-wise it was not quite as dashing as the Thunderbird, but still nothing to be sneezed at, either. A Corvette could be equally as enticing as a T-Bird to any cheerleader. In the beginning, however, the Corvette had been considerably less powerful than the 'T'. With its modified 6 cylinder engine and automatic transmission, it was capable of 150 hp. When Ford came out with the T-Bird in 1955, Chevy made a V-8 optional on the Corvette which boosted the horsepower and kept the 'Vette' in the competition.

There were other dream cars in those years. A convertible of any type was almost a sure-fire guarantee of a red-hot date for Saturday night. They were likewise more expensive, even as used cars. But every once in a while, with some judicious trading, one could acquire a 'flop top.' Almost every manufacturer in those pre-Ralph Nader times offered a convertible. Buick brought out a limited edition sports convertible in 1953. Called the Skylark, it sported Kelsey-Hayes chrome wire wheels and none of the portholes so typical of Buicks at that time. Only 1690 of this particular model were produced and they wore a price tag of $5000. Not exactly a car you could drive home to Mother, but there were many, many others, each unique and special in its own way.

Pontiac, in 1955, came out with its first V-8 engine car, called the Strato-Streak. It was a spunky, if conventional, design capable of 180 hp without the optional four barrel carburetor. Given the optional carburetor, it was easily capable of 200 hp. Moreover, the engine ran on regular gas and had an 8.1 compression ratio. The Star Chief convertible was a knockout in the series. It featured a wraparound windshield, tubeless white side-

Opposite top: How to have a perfect afternoon: your best girl and the Ford Fairlane Sunliner with the top down—the year? 1956.
Opposite bottom: The 1957 Ford Fairlane 500 varied slightly from the Fairlane in trim options and interior decor. There were both the 6 cylinder and the V-8 available on any model.
Above: The 1957 Thunderbird 2-door was a classic in its own time and still is today. In the 50s it was every boy's dream to own one.
Following page: The first Corvette came out in 1953. It was a fiberglass two-seater. As the two on the bicycle could testify, it was a lot more exciting than anything else on the road.

Top: I was a teenage wallflower—until my parents bought the 1953 Ford Sunliner! The Sunliner offered a ready introduction to the most interesting people.

Bottom: The Chevy Bel Air for 1958, a far cry from its 1957 counterpart at the race track but a popular model with the public.

Top: A view of the 1959 Corvette as might be seen by the prospective buyer.

Bottom: Everyone always wants to look under the hood, so here's the same 59 Corvette from a different angle.

Top: A 1957 Pontiac Super Chief Catalina Coupe. (Sometimes the name was longer than the car!)
Bottom: A 1955 Pontiac Wagon. Pontiac's most memorable station wagon was the hardtop-styled Safari, based on the Chevrolet Nomad.

Opposite Top: The 1958 Corvette, swift and sexy, the delight of sports car fans.
Opposite bottom: Corvette in a civilized version for the young executive with playboy fantasies.

CAN-AM
TICKETS: TICKETRON, BASS, MACY'S,
CAPWELLS.
LAGUNA SECA RACEWAY OCT
7-8
MISS SHASTA GRAND PRIX
Shasta
O 58

Bottom: The 1956 Buick Century was one of the fastest Buicks ever built. The Century could go from 0 to 60 mph in 10½ seconds and exceed 110 mph.

Top: A 1957 Chevrolet Bel Air station wagon, big and roomy, just what the suburban matron needed.

Above: Apple orchards and the Chevy to let you take it all in. These were simple pastoral pleasures in 1955.

wall tires, and two-tone paint. It was one to set your sights for.

These were the years when the Drive-In was a new thing. There were drive-in movies, the drive-in root beer stand with its snappy waitresses who delivered an order right to the car, and the drive-in car washes where one could get his car washed, buffed and waxed without ever turning a hand. The car spelled freedom and quiet revolution among the nation's youth. No longer did a boy walk his girl to the movies or spend summer nights sitting in the porch swing holding hands. Now he could be off to anywhere—the beach, the amusement park, downtown, uptown, the drag-races and best of all, the drive-in movie. There were the countless hours he drove up and down main street just to see what was happening or, better yet, to be seen. There were the private drag-races he and his friends had on country roads. It was exciting, it was fun and nobody but the kids understood what it was all about.

There were the Saturday nights after the movies, when no one wanted to go home yet. Everyone would gather at the local hamburger joint and drive 'round and 'round the place yelling mild insults at the fellow ahead. Sometimes it went on for an hour or more, nobody wanting to drop out.

It was a time of warm summer nights, listening to the Beach Boys, gaudy rock 'n' roll bands, a time between the Korean Conflict and the protest marches of the 60s, a time when everyone laid back and had fun. Pollution? Nobody thought of it. Energy Crisis? What was that? Gas was 30 cents a gallon. Steel shortages? Never! It was a time when people had some very old-fashioned ideas about right and wrong, good and bad.

TV was just coming on the scene. Lucille Ball and Desi Arnaz, Kukla, Fran and Ollie, the Honeymooners—sex and violence? Not in the living room.

There was the generation gap, of course. There has always been a generation gap, a boundary between adolescence and adulthood. Driving a car, as your father made plain, involved a good deal of responsibility. Goof up just once, and you'd lose the privilege for a month or so. You knew he meant it. You also knew that he was right. A car, handled recklessly, was dangerous in the extreme. What your own father didn't mention, your girlfriend's father would. She had to be home by 12 o'clock on weekends. You had to come to the house and pick her up, which meant coming in to talk for a while and putting up with smart remarks from her wretched little brother. Her Dad had pretty strict rules: absolutely no drinking at any time, call if you're going to be late, drive safely!

The San Francisco Police Department relied on the faithful Ford squad car in their battle against crime.

Chapter V. Chopped, Channeled and Customized

The sunny, Never-Never Land of California sprouts its own kind of unique Life Style. Fenced off from the rest of the world by mountains on the east and the broad Pacific on the west, California is an island unto itself. In the 50s, it was the place to be. California, synonymous with the good life, golden beaches, suntanned girls, surfing and the Beach Boys. There was a spirit of Youth and Freedom all across the country, which had its roots in these sundrenched beaches. The kids were expressing themselves in ways that kids had never done before. There was that strange blend of music, called rock 'n' roll. There were black leather jackets and ducktail haircuts, flat tops and sunglasses, ponytails and sock-hops. And there were cars—the fins, the chrome, the garish automobiles of the 50s. Kids, ever scornful of the ludicrous, took on the automobile as a kind of artistic expression, a way to poke fun at the world.

It was 'in' to be a nonconformist. The strong silent types like James Dean were the heroes of the day. Wild cars were part of the image. The roaring exhausts and screeching brakes marked a true rebel of the road. There were those who toyed with engines, boring out cylinders and lengthening the stroke. There were others who worked on the exteriors, cutting and welding, painting and striping. One of the latter was George Barris.

Barris had been a child of the Depression. He'd been fascinated by cars then. When he acquired his first car, a 1925 Buick, much the worse for wear, George set

Opposite: The 1954 Mercury inherited Ford's overhead valve V-8. Unlike Ford, Mercury's OHV engine had a greater displacement, thus more power.
Above : A view of the same Mercury from the driver's side. Note spotlight detail. Spotlights furnished the teenage crowd with such simple games as spotlight tag at the local drive-in movies.
Bottom: The 1954 Mercury viewed from the left rear side.

Chevrolet, circa 1950, as American as apple pie, but not even that exciting. Powered by the venerable stovebolt 6 it could cruise all day at 69mph. But woe betide anyone who pushed it to 70.

to work. With care and love, (and probably tongue-in-cheek) he smoothed the dented fenders, sewed up the torn interior, and then, in a burst of exuberance, painted the car orange and blue with diagonal rainbow stripes. Naturally, no one can drive a car like that and not get noticed. George, it seemed, had found the path to instant fame!

His next creation had once been a 1929 Model A Ford. Just for fun, Barris added extra lights to the front of it, strange, winged ornaments and foxtails! To enhance his art, Barris hung around a local body shop. Here, he learned the art of bending and shaping metal, grinding and cutting, torch welding and body paneling. Customizing went into hibernation during World War II. But shortly after the war was over, Barris opened shop again. There weren't too many late-model cars around at the time, so Barris set to work on a '36 Ford convertible.

First he removed the running boards. He molded new taillights, emblems and door handles. And he chopped the top. When a customizer talked about chopping the top, he meant lowering the car's roofline by removing sheet metal. This resulted in a lower profile, a kind of rakish look sometimes, but sometimes it was just plain kooky. There were customers who carried the art of chopping so far that the windshield became only a slit!

Well, it was fun and Barris Kustoms was by now a pretty well-known landmark in the Los Angeles suburb

where he lived. But fame came to the door as a result of the hot rod and custom car show held at the Los Angeles Armory. George's cars appeared in the first issue of a new magazine called *Hot Rod.* Nobody, least of all George Barris, had ever guessed how many people secretly longed to drive a blistering blue automobile with violet flames streaming out from the hood, chrome from ear to ear, and no door handles. Hollywood stars, always looking for something a little different, came to Barris with their fantasies. With a wave of the magic welding torch, there it was, the hot rod Elvis always wanted. Barris built cars for many of the stars: Jayne Mansfield, Tony Curtis, Bobby Darin, and Liberace, among others.

What was curious was that car manufacturers attended the custom shows. They made notes. They drew pictures. Some of these customizers had good ideas. In 1954, Barris brought out the Golden Sahara. It became famous across the nation and drew crowds wherever it was exhibited. The Sahara featured such things as bumper bullets, a checkered grille, thin-line rear fins and a spare tire well molded into the rear decklid. The bumper bullets became famous on the Cadillac. Ford borrowed the checkered grille and the spare tire well appeared on the Chrysler Imperial three years later.

Though George Barris was probably the earliest and best known (he was often called King of the Kustomizers) of the professionals, there were others who became equally famous in their own territory. One of these was Darryl Starbird who got started in his father's home workshop in Wichita, Kansas. Starbird's creations were known for their futuristic styling. Several of his cars sported a bubble top made of contoured plastic, an out-of-this-world design, indeed. One of Starbird's designs featured a double-bubble. It had flip-down doors, three wheels and a single large headlight. It was the closest thing one could get to a flying saucer in the 50s.

Darryl Starbuck won national recognition for his work. In 1959, he received the Top Body Achievement Award at the National Hot Rod Association's National Custom Car Show in Detroit. His entry had been a 1956 Ford Thunderbird restyled in Starbuck's futuristic manner. Starbuck's show cars were given surrealistic names like the Predicta, the Forcasta, the Fantabula—all in character with the outer-space kind of styling they displayed.

What was happening with the customizers at this time was that each was taking pieces of various automobiles and reassembling all these various fins, taillights, grilles and fenders into cars that were totally unlike anything else on the road. Was it simple welding shop finesse or real artistry? Perhaps a little of both went into these incredible pieces of machinery. In the mid-50s, deep in the heart of beautiful downtown Detroit, two very creative brothers named Larry and Mike Alexander operated an establishment they called Custom City. Here they plied their trade, taking the standard production-line car and recreating fantastic chariots whose like had never been seen before. One of the cars they tackled was the 1956 Ford.

The Ford of that year was all right, but really pretty tame looking when you got right down to it. The Alexanders made a new grille of Studebaker shells, and installed a wrap-around front bumper centered in the grille opening. They replaced the headlights with those of an Oldsmobile. It wasn't anything much, compared with the things Darryl Starbuck did, but it was nice, the lines were clean and the workmanship was impeccable. The car was chosen by a national magazine as one of the 10 best customs to be built in 1956. The Alexanders had achieved a small measure of greatness and a lot of business for Custom City.

Another West Coast artist was Gene Winfield, who hailed from Modesto, California. Windy got caught for a tour of duty during the Korean Conflict, but that didn't matter. He and a like-minded friend continued customizing even while stationed in Japan. By 1955, Windy was back in the States and going strong once more. His sleek, clean-swept cars took awards left and right at the custom shows. One of Winfield's most radical cars was a revamped 1949 Mercury. It had inlaid bumpers, sculptured wheel wells, quad vertical headlights that were molded in to the fenders, a tubular "floating" grille, and the front seat swung out when the car door was opened. The name of this imaginative modification was the Solar Scene.

When Darryl Starbuck opened his shop in Wichita, he worked with another young customizer named Bill Cushenbery. Cushenbery was soon infected with California fever and went West to Monterey. Here he created one of the outstanding customs of the era. The original car had been a 1940 Ford coupe. Cushenbery chopped the top and sectioned the body to form a very low profile. Called El Matador, the car featured canted, quad headlights and a rolled-pan, contoured rear body section. It was, however the very low silhouette that made the car so exciting.

There were a whole series of 'art forms' that grew up around the business of customizing. Each customizer had his specialty. Paint was one thing that first caught the eye. There were the wild metallic colors that seemed to have unlimited depth. There were fanciful trims like pin-striping. Pin-striping, delicate, swirling, undulating lines that fanned across hood, around windows, headlights, trunks, was the mark of an artist. Pin-striping evolved into flame painting. Flames started out as little flickers shooting out from the hood. Like wild-fire, the idea caught on and the flames spread to engulf the entire car. A real artist, using a range of colors from yellow through brilliant orange-red, could make the flames look almost real. This kind of work took hours of time. Patient blending of colors and hand rubbing were required to get exactly the right touch. The flames then evolved into scalloping.

Scalloping was more subdued than the flames. It was more stylized, more elegant. Done with care, by a consummate artist, scalloping would not have looked much out of place on the local banker's car.

So much for the painters. The metalworkers were artists in another media. They worked with cutting tools and welding torches. The cars they produced reveal a lot about the 50s. There was a sense of fun, of fantasy and sometimes a little tongue-in-cheek humor. Just imagine a 1950 Ford coupe with the following embellishments: quad headlights; taillights from a '57 Olds 98; floating grille; exhaust pipes that extend along the side rocker panels; no door handles; everything smooth, sculpted, and clean. The color of the car is deep wine red. Inside, everything is padded in wine and white vinyl. The trunk is padded in the same white vinyl and carpeted with wine red carpeting. Nestled in the recesses of the trunk is a TV so you need not miss American Bandstand while on your picnic. The TV operates on a voltage converter. This, remember, was before the age of the portable TV.

Customizing was a kind of 'bits and pieces' operation in one sense. First there was the basic car, say a 1950 Chevrolet. Dull, very dull and very ordinary. But how would it look with a different grille? A customizer might take the grille teeth from a '53 Chevy and install them in a molded-in grille shell. This was better, but only a beginning.

The headlights were the next thing to go. Installed in their place were a pair of lights from a '55 Oldsmobile.

Above: A 1955 Chevy done in a metallic green fleck paint job. Blue flames coming from the hood were the finishing touch of the customizer's art.

Next the hood was 'nosed' and slightly reshaped. (Nosing was a term which meant all chrome, including hood ornaments had been removed and all the holes had been filled in.) Then the car would be channeled. (Channeled referred to the lowering of a car's body within the frame so that it appeared to be floating over the ground.)

Chromed exhaust pipes running from the front wheel along the side of the car to the rear wheel were another touch many customizers added. For taillights, how about those of a '54 Mercury, inverted and mounted low in the rear fenders? And for further interest, the rear would be decked. (Decking meant that all the rear trim and chrome would be removed and again, all the holes would be filled.)

Much of the customizer's art lay in attention to details. Unusual hub caps, bumpers, skirts on the rear wheel wells, and pleated upholstery added to the one-of-a kind look. The final touch was, of course, the paint job. Metallic paints and lacquers took hours of painstaking labor. Purple was a color much in vogue, because it was so different. Candy-apple red was another. Add flames, scalloping, pinstriping, even cartooning and you had a unique automobile.

Customizing was a labor of love. It took hours to complete each modification, particularly if you chose to do the work yourself. In the 50s, a great many people did their own customizing because of the expense of a professional job and because it was fun. Customizing your own automobile might take three or four years and several thousand dollars. But the results were worth every minute of time. Driving around in such a car made you king of the hill with all your friends and a superhero with all the cheerleaders.

In a way, customizing was a kind of recycling process, using as it did, so many parts and accessories from various cars. The auto graveyards of America were a customizer's gold mine. With cutting torch, wrench, screwdriver, and a little pocket money, you could obtain enough 'goodies' to produce any fantasy you had in mind. The exhilaration of a visit to the local junk yard was matched only by being invited to participate in the Saturday night drag races.

Though some forms of customizing were really on the wild side with extravagant shapes, colors and interiors, much of it, at least in the early and mid-50s was rather conservative. Much of it was also a vast improvement over the original styling. (Probably that was the reason so many auto designers attended the custom shows and made notes.) In view of the art forms of the 60s, i.e, Andy Warhol's Campbell's Soup, etc, what the customizers did with the automobile was really a forerunner of pop art.

Chapter VI. Daytona, Bonneville and Points South

Americans, from time immemorial, have loved racing. Horse racing must have been one of the earliest sports in the Colonies, since wagering on the races was so often a punishable offense. Every 19th century county fair had its horse races and there were more than a few impromptu 'races' by stalwart and respectable deacons and pious church members on Sunday mornings in those early days.

The very first gasoline-powered automobile ever to chug down the road in the United States was built by the Duryea brothers from Illinois. It was the summer of 1893 when this marvel came to pass–and pass very slowly, at that. With its four horsepower, one cylinder engine and its weight of 750 pounds, the car moved at an easy walking pace! But time passed and the car, with modifications and improvements, could travel all of ten miles an hour. Three years after its first slow appearance, the Duryea went into production. In that year, 1896, 10 of the 'horseless carriages' were sold to intrepid buyers. It was an era of inventors, however, and a great many people were probing the possibilities of the motor car.

The first automobile race occurred on 22 July 1894 in France. News of the race fired American auto builders to emulate it. The first American race ever was sponsored by H H Kohlsaat, the publisher of the Chicago *Times-Herald.* The date for the race was Thanksgiving Day, 1895; the starting time was 9 am. Six cars made it to the starting line which was blanketed in heavy snow. During the race three cars broke down, one collided with a horse-drawn hack and one driver passed out from the cold. A Duryea, despite losing its way and breaking down, managed to finish the race–to win it, even. The official time was 54 miles in 10 hours and 23 minutes. One other car, a German Benz, completed that momentous race, an hour and a half behind the Duryea. Automobile racing in America was born on that cold, snowy, November day.

Racing has been important all along in the development of the automobile. Not because of the prizes, but because of the recognition that winners receive. As Henry Ford once said, 'Winning or making a record was the best kind of advertising.' By the early 1900's all kinds of auto racing flourished. People held races on city streets, converted horse tracks and on country roads. Record breaking was equally popular for a time. Hill climbing events like Pikes Peak, Eagle Rock and Mt Washington spurred adventurous drivers to try their luck. The first race at the Indianapolis Speedway was held in 1909. Pioneer auto manufacturers used the event to promote sales of their cars. But they were not alone. All the industry suppliers, the tire companies, the makers of shock absorbers, carburetors and headlights used the racing triumphs as promotional material.

Racing continued in the United States through the 20s and even the dismal times of the 30s. During World War II, racing all but ceased.

In the late 40s, a gas station attendant named Bill France decided to devote his talents to developing the sport of stock car racing. In addition to being a mechanic, Bill had often done some stock car racing on the side.

Stock car racing, in those days, was mainly confined to the Southeastern states. There was a good and interesting reason for this. Stock car racing had its roots in the honored Southern tradition of 'moonshining.' It was a foregone fact that the local bootleggers had long held the advantage over the government 'revenuers', knowing as they did every uncharted backroad and byway in the county. But tax-collecting has always been one of the more imaginative branches of the government. And 'revenuers' by their very nature, were among the more sporting types of bureaucrats.

To improve their odds at catching the rum-runners, the Government men developed some very crafty automobiles. The word got around. The opposition, naturally, did some very fancy tinkering of its own. Local mechanics probed the possibilities of the factory-built engine. It is hard to believe that sport didn't play as much a part in this as the lucrative business of moonshining. Delivering moonshine served as a training ground for some of the early stock car drivers. All the techniques of evasion, highspeed turns, power slides, and braking were present in running moonshine.

Bill France, who'd done some of the engine work as well as driving in stock car races, set about to regulate specifications for stock cars and improve benefits for drivers. In 1946, France asked the AAA Contest Board

Opposite: Edsel Ford (left) chatting with Edward H Armstrong, Mayor of Daytona Beach, Florida. Daytona owes much of its fame to the Daytona time trials.

Above: The lady's choice: a pink and white 1956 Chrysler convertible. Automobile companies were well aware that she got to pick the color.
Opposite: The 1955 Chrysler was known as the 100 million dollar look.

to sanction a 100 mile championship stock car race at Charlotte, North Carolina. The board declined to sanction the race, so in December of 1947 Bill France and a group of stock car fans formed the National Association for Stock Car Racing—known ever since as NASCAR.

NASCAR caught the imagination of racing fans in the 50s. There was a kind of democracy in stock car racing that didn't exist elsewhere. Grassroots Americans have always been a little suspicious of things European. Here was an American kind of race with American cars driven by good old boys from back home. None of those temperamental Italian cars (though, of course, it was impossible to keep the Ferraris out completely). But the excitement of these races came from the showings of such cars as the Buick Century, the Olds 88 and Chrysler 300—all the pride of Detroit. Drivers like Fireball Roberts and the father and son team Lee and Richard Petty were revered folk heroes.

In the South, particularly, stock car racing preempted both baseball and football as the most popular sport. The popularity spread in the 50s from the hills of East Tennessee, the North Carolina back-country, all the way to Kansas, Oklahoma and points West. Every little rural town boasted of Friday night stock car races. It kept the kids off the street, and it also enthralled their elders. Adolescents of the 50s found the stocks a perfect way to exercise the urge to tinker with an engine and to race legally. Winners could count on being the hometown hero—at least until the next race. Some of the racers graduated to bigger and better things. Gordon Johncock, who started out in stock car races in Michigan and Indiana went on to the Indianapolis Speedway. Stocks were exciting; perhaps more so than the 'big' races, because so many ordinary people were personally involved.

What should be emphasized about all cars of the 50s is that they were big, heavy automobiles in comparison with today's cars. They featured heavy frames and bodies of heavy-gauge steel. To think of such hulks on the race track seems ludicrous. The engines for these monsters, however, were built for power and performance. And perform, they did, with breath-taking ability. Chrysler's hemi-head V-8 was a notorious power plant. Some racers who modified the hemi were able to get as much as 1,000 hp (for very short periods) from the lion-hearted engine. The Chrysler 300, born in 1955, dominated NASCAR racing in the mid-50s.

Cadillac would certainly never be considered a racing car, or would it? The 1950 series 61 was a relatively light car which came equipped with standard transmission and a 160 V-8 engine. According to some drivers, it was the fastest passenger car in the US at that time. Proof might be seen in the results of the LeMans for 1950. A near-stock Coupe de Ville and a Cadillac equipped with a special body came in 10th and 11th, overall. An Allard J2, powered by the same Cadillac V-8 engine, came in third. Racing did not really fit the Cadillac image,

though. So Cadillac engines often raced in the bodies of other cars. Fordillac and Studillac were two hybrids designed by Bill Frick. (Briggs Cunningham and Phil Walters once 'stuffed' a Cadillac engine into an Austin-Healy. The resulting automobile took a first and second at Watkins Glen! Thereupon, Cadillac refused to sell Cunningham any more engines.)

There were other cars whose manufacturers weren't so stuffy about 'prestige'. The Buick Century was one and the Olds 88 was another. The Hudson Hornet, a rather ugly, if aerodynamically sound, automobile was outstanding in AAA and NASCAR racing until the mid-50s. The Hudson Hornet was an interesting car from the standpoint of stock car racing. The Hornet came equipped with a brawny 308 cubic inch (5.0L) 6 cylinder engine. With its 3.8x4.5 bore and stroke, it was capable of something like 145 bhp at 3800 rpm in stock form. But in the hands of a precision tuner it was capable of much more.

Such a tuner was Marshall Teague. Teague claimed he could get 112 mph from a certified 'stock' Hornet. Aided by Hudson engineers, Teague proved his ideas in the 1952 AAA season, which he finished with a 1,000 point lead over his nearest rival. Engineers at Hudson, fired with enthusiasm for Teague's ideas, had introduced a series of 'severe usage' options which were actually nothing more than disguised racing modifications. Twin H-power, which was offered for the first time in 1953, consisted of twin carburetors and dual manifold induction, never before offered on a 6. The 7-X racing engine arrived late in 1953. Modifications included over-bored cylinders (.020) a special cam and head, larger valves and higher compression. 7-X was just what Marshall Teague needed. A true racing engine, 7-X was capable of 210 bhp. In that year, 1953, NASCAR drivers like Herb Thomas, Frank Mundy, Al Keller and Dick Rathmann won 21 races driving the modified Hornet.

In those years, very few cars outran the Hudson Hornet. One that came close was the Chrysler Saratoga. The stock Saratoga, with its powerful hemi engine could make 0 to 60 in 10 seconds. Flat out, it could achieve 110 mph, a ferocious competitor for the Hornet . . . but not quite good enough. But then came the big 300 in 1955, which delivered 300 bhp as a modified stock engine. The Chrysler 300 was a legend in NASCAR racing in those years. It probably would have remained a dominant force in NASCAR if the Automobile Manufacturers Association had not decided to de-emphasize racing.

Another of the powerful sedans that took to racing was the Oldsmobile. Engineers introduced the first Rocket 88 engine in 1949. The Rocket 88 was one of those landmark designs so typical of the 50s. It was so far ahead of its time that even today, 30 years later, most large American cars are powered by engines like the Rocket 88. Specifications for the engine include 303.7 cubic inch (5.0L) displacement, compression ratio of between 7.5:1 and 8:1 (up to 12:1 with the right kind of octane), over-square bore and stroke of 3.75 x 3.44 inches and a torque of 240 foot-pounds initially. Oldsmobile had originally planned to use the Rocket only in the Olds 98 model, but the division general manager, Sherrod Skinner, opted for using the engine in the 88 as

Above: Cars of the Big Run drive up California Street in San Francisco at the conclusion of their 51,000 mile course. Another fantastic 50s phenomenon. The time is May 10, 1957.

well. The Rocket in the lighter 88 was a natural for NASCAR racing. As a stock car, the Olds 88 proved itself in no uncertain terms. In its first year of competition, the 88 was entered in nine NASCAR grand nationals. Of those nine, the Olds 88s won six. At the Daytona Time Trials in 1950, an 88 broke the speed record for its class with a two-way average speed of 100.28 mph.

There were other races in the 50s. One that has been nearly hidden by the mists of time was called officially the Carrera Panamericana. To aficionados and racing drivers, it was known more simply as the Mexican Road Race. It was international in scope and covered a distance of 2,178 miles the year it was first run (1950). It was won that first year by an Oldsmobile 88 driven by Hershel McGriff. McGriff's average speed was 77.43 miles per hour. Running against such formidable European contenders as Alfa-Romeo, the Olds had truly proved itself in this grueling race. In the following years, the course was shortened to a distance of 1,934 miles. The strong and durable Lincoln, with its innovative ball-joint front suspension dominated those rugged miles. Running in the International Standard Class, Lincolns had no peer. Lincolns took the top five places in the Mexican in 1952. In 1953, this so-called luxury sedan picked up the top four places and in 1954, a first and second place.

Today, the thought of such an automobile competing in a road race at all is laughable. The fact that Lincoln won and won consistently, is incredible. How was it possible? Part of it was due to the superior valve-in-head V-8 engine. An even larger part was due to the race preparation Lincolns received.

Clay Smith was a mechanic with a magic touch. It was his job to 'prep' the Lincolns for the arduous Mexican Road Race. The Ford Motor Company, eager for the publicity that winning the race would bring, had none of the compunctions about prestige that Cadillac suffered. After obtaining Smith's services as a mechanic, the company went all out to see that he had the best materials to work with. Thus, Lincolns were equipped with 'export' suspension, Ford truck camshafts, mechanical valve lifters, special hubs and front wheel spindles. To this list was also added the choice of two optional rear ends. What is truly incredible, is that Lincoln, equipped with a higher axle and a stock engine, could top 130 mph! Chuck Stevenson, who won the race in 1952, finished nearly an hour ahead of the Ferrari which had won the race the year before. Clay Smith was killed in a tragic pit accident in 1954. It was the last year of the Mexican.

What is little known about the Mexican Road Race is that in addition to Oldsmobile and Lincoln, Dodge was

Above: George Alsbury (left) with his Chrysler New Yorker, and Mel Alsbury with his Imperial in Galveston, Texas, at the conclusion of the 1958 Mobilgas Economy Run. The late 50s saw less emphasis on speed and racing and more on fuel economy.

another outstanding American car. In that last year, 1954, Dodge took over the Medium Stock class. Dodge, noted for its high-efficiency engine, took 1-2-3-4-6-9 positions, an excellent record for such a difficult marathon.

Not much is written or remembered of the Mexican Road Race now. But in those years of the early 50s, when racing was gaining a foothold in the public's imagination, the Carrera-Panamericana represented all the glamour and hard-driving a race could be.

Daytona Beach, Florida has been associated with automobiles and racing since 1902, when Alexander Winton and RE Olds first raced on the sands of Ormond-Daytona. The brief 15-mile stretch of sand established Daytona as the place to try for land speed records. Daytona held sway for nearly 30 years, until racers discovered the salt flats of Utah.

City fathers in Daytona viewed with alarm the mass Western Exodus. In 1936, Sig Haugdahl, a former Daytona record-holder, was called in to offer suggestions. Daytona, after all, was a tourist attraction. Tourists meant cash money. The city fathers didn't want to see a good thing die.

Haugdahl's solution was amazingly simple. Take 1½ miles of sandy beach plus 1½ miles of parallel blacktop highway and join each section by a one-tenth mile connecting road. What do you get? Roughly an oval track running about 3 and 2/10 miles. With a little advertising and a $5000 purse, the Daytona Track lured an Indianapolis winner, Bill Cummings; a couple of dirt track stars, Doc Mackenzie and Bob Sall; a British race driver, Major Goldie Gardiner; midget auto racing champion Bill Schindler and a young Virginian named Bill France.

The AAA Board had sanctioned a 250 mile race. But the city fathers had forgotten one thing; with all the 'heavy traffic,' the two connecting roads soon became impossible and impassable. The race was called at 200 miles when the overworked tow trucks could no longer dislodge all the stranded vehicles fast enough to keep the course open. Such was the running of the first Daytona stock car race.

With the end of World War II, Daytona Speed Week came into full bloom. There was a new track, a few miles south of the 1936 landmark. It included, as did the old track, a combination beach and highway course running a distance of 4.1 miles. Time trials were again being held on the beach as in the early days of automobile racing. Speed Week occurred in February. Running the Daytona Time Trials became an important part of winter vacation for many race car enthusiasts. After all, the formal straightaway runs, NASCAR allowed the tourists a moment of glory. For the sum of 12 dollars, you could take your own Chrysler hemi or hot Buick on an officially timed run across the sand. Those who recorded better than 100 mph became members of the Century

Ford
CALIFORNIA
DOCS26T
LET'S BOOGIE!

Opposite: The customized car came into its own in the 50s. This was partly a reaction to the extreme styles Detroit was turning out. But it also reflected the preoccupation kids had with cars.
Top: A 1952 Oldsmobile Super 88. It was stodgy in appearance but what made the difference was under the hood. The 88s were long and powerful cars; this particular model had a 120″ wheelbase and horsepower that ranged around 160.
Bottom: A 1954 Lincoln Capri convertible. While Lincoln was a true luxury car, its performance in the Mexican Road Race (Carrera Panamericana) was phenomenal.

Club. Nothing could have done more to fire the public's enthusiasm for Daytona.

Speed Week in the mid-50s was dominated by NASCAR entries. The 1955 Grand National was won by Tim Flock, driving a Chrysler 300. Flock's closest competitor was Lee Petty, also driving a Chrysler. Third place went to a Buick Century, followed by two Olds 88s for fourth and fifth. Fireball Roberts, driving another Buick, had appeared to dominate the race. NASCAR officials, however, declared Robert's car illegal since the push rods had been altered. The track by now was known as the Daytona 500. As one of the best known tracks of that era, it regularly drew crowds of 100 thousand or better.

Stock car racing had really come of age at this point and much of its prestige was due to the efforts of Bill France. As previously mentioned, France had been both a mechanic and a race driver since the early 30s. Stock car racing in those years before the second World War had grown rapidly and had gotten out of hand. Under the chaotic conditions which existed then, drivers were at the mercy of unscrupulous promoters who would often 'skip town' with the gate receipts, leaving behind

Top: Sir Malcolm Campbell (right) is congratulated by Ted Allen of the American Automobile Association on the certification of his 272 mph speed record at Daytona Beach 1933 February 27.
Bottom: Sir Malcolm Campbell at the wheel. Campbell's exploits as a landspeed record holder were to inspire many drivers of the 50s.

unpaid bills and drivers' purses. Some mechanics, also, belonged to a slippery bunch who knew how to cheat the drivers for profit. Safety standards and rules were rarely well-enforced. It was to combat these conditions and to give the sport of stock car racing respectability, that Bill France founded NASCAR. France set out to clean up and promote stock car racing in the late 40s.

The first superspeedway built especially for NASCAR races was opened in Darlington, South Carolina in 1950. The track, 1⅜ miles long with high banked turns, was eyed pessimistically by many. Who would want to travel to a little hick-town on the outskirts of nowhere just to see a 500 mile race; could any of the entrants last 500 miles? Nevertheless, NASCAR'S first 500 miler was run in Darlington and was, despite all misgivings, quite successful. Darlington, along with Daytona, Charlotte, Rockingham, Atlanta and Talladega became one of the outstanding of NASCAR'S superspeedways.

Speed records have always been a part of racing. In the early days, before and after World War I, it was the sandy Daytona Beach strip that provided an area for land speed records. It is hard to believe that 75 years ago when automobiles were still in their infancy, Frank Marriott, driving a Stanley Steamer with what look like over-sized bicycle tires, broke the land speed record at 129 mph. But this was nothing at all, when compared to the records set by the daring Malcolm Campbell in his famous Bluebird. Sir Malcolm's exploits will be legendary for as long as speed records are attempted.

In 1935, the speed record was 276.82 mph. Sir Malcolm made his first run over the famous Salt Flats at Bonneville, Utah late in 1935. On his first run, he established a speed in excess of 300 mph. Campbell was to break many land speed records at Bonneville and, by 1947, the land speed record at Bonneville was 400 mph. Sir Malcolm died in 1949, having held the land speed record nine different times throughout his career. Memories of the Bluebird and her daring driver served as inspiration for a new generation of record breakers.

Above: The 1951 Buick Model 48D. Buick was well-known for a tradition of quality and high performance.

But what about California? Was the mecca of automania out of the racing picture? Decidedly not, but it took a different twist. Stock car racing never achieved the popularity there that it did in the South and Midwest.

What happened was that the West Coast invented its own unique form of organized racing—drag racing. Drag racing is unlike either stock car racing or sports car racing. The cars run two at a time, side by side. It's a standing-start contest between evenly matched cars, the sole objective being to see which car crosses a finish line 1,320 feet away first. It takes a certain type of person to enjoy these races. The race is over in a few seconds and often no one is able to see the finish, due to the dust and smoke. Yet nearly 8 million fans pay to attend these races every year.

Drag racing in the 50s was only a half-serious sport. Kids of the 50s couldn't resist the lure of speed. They puttered around in their free time, combining automobile chassis and frames with V-8 engines in the hope of coming up with the ultimate fast car. Racing such cars on public thoroughfares, as they sometimes did, was dangerous. Rather than totally discourage drag racing, Wally Parks and several others civilized it instead. Founding the National Hot Rod Association (NHRA), Parks organized drag meets on unused airport runways. The runways were about one half to three quarters of a mile long. Since a quarter of a mile was nearly the limit a driver could accelerate and still stop safely within the bounds of the runway, it became the established distance for drag racing.

Chapter VII. The Cream of the Crop

Never before in automotive history had designers and engineers been so innovative. There was great freedom to experiment and to develop new ideas. Competition was keen among the manufacturers. The model changeover was a time of high excitement for everyone. It was called by its detractors, 'planned obsolescence': the idea, real or imagined, that last year's automobile could not hold a candle to this year's new model. Thus one manufacturer might come up with an excellent design, but three years was the maximum time that design would be produced—more likely it would only be on the market for two years before another major restyling.

There were cars in these years that were classic in their beauty. Cars so incredibly sculpted, so sleek and clean-lined that they invite admiration and even imitation today. One of these classics was the Studebaker Loewy Coupe.

Studebaker was the oldest automobile manufacturer in the nation. The company had been in business since the time of horse-drawn carriages. 1952 was a centennial birthday for the South Bend company. Car sales had been falling for the independent company. The manufacturer blamed it on the Korean War restrictions. But that was probably only the tip of the iceberg so far as internal problems were concerned. Clearly the company needed a car that would boost its sagging sales.

For the 1953 model year, Raymond Loewy's design studios introduced the Commander and Champion, Starliner hardtop and Starlight coupe. The designs were those of chief designer, Robert E Bourke, who had intended them as a special show model at first. Loewy, impressed with the design, sold it to the Studebaker management who adopted the style for their '53 model. The lines of these cars were faultless. Having none of the garish chrome or over-done trim, none of the boxy lines so typical of its competitors, the Starlight/Starliners were elegantly simple with a European look. These cars would be lauded as the outstanding automotive design of the decade.

Unfortunately, Studebaker experienced a delay in production due to model changeover. When they finally did get underway, it was discovered that management had read the market wrong. Demand for the magnificent coupe was four times greater than for the sedan which management had thought would be the top

Below: A 1956 Continental Mark II. It is tempting to call this car a Lincoln Continental, however, Continental was a separate division of the Ford Motor Company. The Mark II is known as one of the world's great classic cars.
Opposite top: The 1957 Continental Mark II was renowned for its flawless styling. The $10,000 price tag, however did not appeal to buyers.
Opposite bottom: The Continental Mark III for 1958 was garish by comparison.

CH 2878

1952
1108
CALIFORNIA

seller. It took weeks to switch over to production of the coupe and much valuable time and many sales were lost.

The series was offered again for the model year 1954, the only change being the egg-crate grille. But production woes still besieged the company. Less than 70,000 cars were produced for the entire year. Problems lay with management and cost of production. Robert Bourke, as a matter of curiosity, priced out one of his Commander Starliners according to the cost used by General Motors. The results were shocking. Had the Commander been a Chevrolet, it would have sold for $1900. As a Studebaker, it was selling for $2502. These were the years in which a price war was being fought between Ford and GM. Neither company really injured the other, but it was the small independents who suffered irretrievable losses. Packard, at this time, bought out Studebaker and the company became known as Studebaker-Packard. The rest is history. The classic 'Loewy Coupes' stand yet as a reminder of the excellence that was possible in the era of fins and chrome.

The Ford Motor Company had long produced a model called the Lincoln Continental, a luxurious car much beloved by many dealers and customers alike. But the Lincoln Continentals died in 1948 and there seemed little likelihood that they would ever be reborn. Then in the mid-fifties, due to much pressure from dealers and customers, Ford brought out a separate division called simply Continental. In developing the Continental, Ford's goal was to establish dominance in the high-priced field of automobiles, and especially to dominate Cadillac.

The year was 1956, when the first Continental cost was 10,000 dollars. Ten thousand dollars of perfection, flawless in every line and exquisitely built—that was the Mark II. It was the only model Continental produced for that year and the following year. The lines were crisp, slightly rakish, clean and elegant. It had been three years in development. The project, under the direction of William Clay Ford, (Henry Ford II's younger brother) had called in a distinguished group of consultants to submit their ideas. They were Buzz Grisinger, Reese Miller, Vince Gardener, George Walker (who later became Ford's design chief) and Walter Buell Ford (no relation to *the* Fords). Their designs were nice, but somehow they were just not right.

In the end, the management reviewed 13 different presentations before they finally selected a design from Reinhart, Buehrig, and Thomas of Special Products. The car was regal in its simplicity. Harley Copp, who was chief engineer for Special Products, drew up a special Chassis frame of steel rails. They dipped low be-

Left: Miss Studebaker poses on top of San Francisco's Nob Hill with the Class 2 winner of the Mobilgas Economy Run. With her are a group of Northern California district Studebaker dealers.

Top: A classic car in the tradition of the great Duesenberg was the Continental Mark II of 1957. Lack of sales brought about a new design and the classic Mark II faded into the sunset.

Bottom: Though it sold better, the Continental Mark III lacked the simple elegance of its predecessor, the Mark II. The 1958 Mark III was based on the Lincoln design with an incredible 131″ wheelbase.

Top: The 1956 Packard Executive, shown here in the hardtop model with two-tone paint. Executive appeared in the middle of the model year, 1956. It bridged the gap between the Clipper and Packard.

Bottom: An inside look at the same 1956 Packard Executive. New for this year was the push button transmission. Notice the Clipper logo on the horn.

The newest of the new!

Advanced '55 Studebaker

NEW VISIBILITY! NEW COLOR! NEW POWER! NO INCREASE IN PRICES!

Windows that raise or lower—automatically!
These advanced new 1955 Studebakers offer the newest of the new in electrically controlled door windows—a convenience available for either the front-door windows only, or for all doors, as you prefer.

Here is America's newest surprise from alert, fast-moving Studebaker—a breath-taking additional line of 1955 Studebakers!

Here is unexpected new Studebaker visibility . . . dramatic new two-toning that accentuates the Studebaker speedlined look . . . tremendously increased new lightning-fast Studebaker power!

You get all this at no increase in Studebaker's low-level competitive prices! Marvelous power assists and air-conditioning, as pictured, are optional at extra cost. See your Studebaker dealer now. Studebaker . . . so much better made . . . worth more when you trade!

Newest of the new air-conditioning!
Studebaker's advanced-design air-conditioning provides more cooling than 10 average home refrigerators—filters, dehumidifies and constantly freshens the air. Optional in Commander and President sedans.

Newest of the new power seats!
Just touch a finger-tip switch and the driver's seat moves forward or backward as desired. This convenience is optional in all Studebakers including Champions.

Safest, surest-stopping power brakes!
A slight pivot of your foot from accelerator to brake pedal—and Studebaker's newest of the new power brakes stop your car swiftly, smoothly, surely. Optional in all 1955 Studebaker models. World's largest brake linings per pound of car!

Newest of the new in ease of parking and steering!
Studebaker power steering—advanced again for 1955—relieves you from tiresome and exasperating wheel tugging. Better still, its price has recently been reduced. Almost everyone can now afford its welcome extra convenience and peace of mind.

See Studebaker-Packard's TV Reader's Digest . . . a new weekly feature on ABC-TV network

STUDEBAKER DIVISION OF THE STUDEBAKER-PACKARD CORPORATION
. . . WORLD'S 4TH LARGEST FULL-LINE PRODUCER OF CARS AND TRUCKS

tween the wheels, allowing the car to have chair-height seats, but at the same time keeping the roofline relatively low. Cockpit and dash were inspired by aircraft designs, sharply delineated and devoid of ornament. The engine was the Lincoln 368 cubic-inch V-8 (6.0L) capable of 285 to 300 horse power at 4600 rpm. The car measured 218.5 inches and rode on a 126 inch wheelbase. It attracted wide-eyed admiration in both Europe and America, a car truly in a class by itself.

But despite its classic beauty, the Continental Mark II was not a blazing success in the market place. The word from the sales division was that Mark II had not made a difference in production. While a few wealthy customers had switched to the Mark II, many more, with less cash, were still buying the rival Cadillac instead of Lincolns. There were price cuts to boost sales. There were Mark III's, Mark IV's and Mark V's. None had the lines or the beauty of the original Mark II. Some sold a little better. The Continental division faded quietly with the 50s. The Mark II Continental, a car on a par with the great Duesenberg, will be remembered always as one of the outstanding automobiles of the decade.

Packard was a car with a reputation. Throughout the 20s and into the 30s, Packard had been one of the outstanding luxury cars. People remembered with nostalgia the Packard Speedster model 734, a sparky roadster which retailed in 1929 for $5,210. It was definitely not a car for the masses. But luxury cars in the Great Depression were hit hard and the Packard Company suffered huge losses. To carry the company along, the management switched to building less expensive cars. This policy continued after World War II, unfortunately.

The Packard of the early 50s was described as a 'pregnant elephant.' The design was a heavy and ungainly pre-war style, not attractive and not popular. For 1951, the company went for total restyling, employing John Reinhart (who would later be remembered for the Mark II Continental). The lines were elegant; far and away from the bulbous '51 model. Though the company still maintained its low-priced line, some of the models being built at this time were reflective of the wonderful old luxury cars. These were the 250's, the 300's and the 400's.

Basically, they were what their forerunners had been, well-built, ultimately comfortable, high-powered road cars. The 300's and 400's were mounted on 127-inch wheelbase, the 250's used the shorter 122-inch wheelbase for the Mayfair hardtop and convertible. The 250's were sporty cars which had a lot of appeal for the public. But despite all, something of the aura had gone. The Packard, once associated with wealthy millionaires, had somehow lost class.

Opposite: An ad for the Studebaker of 1955. This model has been called a technological wonder. Unfortunately, it fell victim to production line tie-ups and problems with quality control.

James Nance became president of Packard in 1952. It was hoped by one and all that Nance could invigorate the flagging company. Nance wanted to return to the days of the luxury formal sedans and limousines. The low-priced 200 models he proposed to turn into a separate line called the Clipper. Clippers came out as a separate make in 1956. In 1953, Packard brought out the Patrician which featured a leather-covered top and tiny rear windows, plus an equally elegant interior. The Patrician sold for $6,531, a price that ranked it with luxury cars like Cadillac and Lincoln. In that same year, the Caribbean, an elegant convertible, beautifully styled, was also introduced. Limited to 750 cars, the Caribbean outsold Cadillac's rival model, the Eldorado.

Packard might well have regained its old glory, had the company not purchased the waning Studebaker plant in South Bend. Packard, at this point, though small, was healthy. Studebaker, on the other hand, was plagued with problems, the largest being high-overhead and low productivity.

Nevertheless, in 1955, Packard brought out a car that was a technological marvel. A top feature was Torsion-Level suspension which consisted of an interlinked torsion bar system that operated on all four wheels. The suspension could correct for any load, thanks to a complex electrical system and the interlinking torsion bar. The ride such a system delivered was like velvet and the handling was in true Packard character. Moreover, there was the new and powerful V-8 engine.

Even on the little Clipper, the engine displacement was 320 cubic inches (5.2L). On the Packards, the displacement was 352. The Ultramatic Transmission, combined with the new V-8 and Torsion-Level suspension, made an excellent drive train. The Caribbean, capable of 275 hp, was an infinitely powerful car. Equal to all this was the styling. A careful facelift of Reinhart's 1951 design, the 1955 Packard wore 'cathedral' taillights, peaked front fenders and a somewhat ornate grille. It was a car in the remembered tradition. But unfortunately there were production line tie-ups and problems with quality control, all very detrimental to sales. Packard was dying. But as a signature to a long, grand history, the 1955 model was a reflection of the glorious past.

The Hudson was a strange amalgam of ugliness and absolute comfort. Probably the original 'wide body,' the Hudson was one car that one stepped down into when entering it. You would be impressed immediately by the broad, chair-height seats which seemed to engulf you in their luxurious depths. Despite its low, ground-hugging style there was plenty of head room in the Hudson—plenty of head room and leg room and stretchout room. In short, it was as if the parlor sofa had been picked up and installed in a car. Never mind that the outside was an uninspiring bulge, few other cars boasted such comfort as this. Say what you wanted about its uninspired exterior, the Hudson, slab-sided and bulky, was extremely aerodynamic for its time.

Chapter VIII. Hot Wheels

Speed was a by-word of the 50s. In retrospect, it is sometimes hard to understand why. The average driver had no real need for a car that would run at speeds in excess of 80 miles per hour. But there it was, the public craved speed and that was what they got. Several cars were notoriously fast. Sometimes those of a certain model year gained a reputation as speed-demons. One such was the 1958 DeSoto Firedome.

DeSoto was one of Chrysler's lines, a fine basic family car in the early 50s. In those years, all De Sotos had 6 cylinder engines, running from 236.7 to 250.6 (2.7-4 OL) cubic inches. Maximum horsepower was about 116. Then in 1952, DeSoto came out with the hemi-head Firedome V-8 engine which developed 160 hp at 4400 rpm. This was the first step in the evolution of DeSoto as a real powerhouse automobile. The Firedome V-8 outsold DeSoto's other models by a margin of 2 to 1. No one needed further proof that the Firedome was a step in the right direction. Horsepower climbed with each succeeding model year, from 160 in 1952 to 230 and 255 in 1956 when it seemed that the engineers must have reached the limit of engine performance. The next year the top of the line would deliver 290 hp while the lowest priced model, the Firesweep, buzzed along with a conservative 260 hp.

1958, however was the pinnacle year for the DeSoto. They featured a fast-shifting TorqueFlite automatic transmission and torsion bar suspension. The Firedome with optional 305 engine, could go from 0 to 60 in 7.7 seconds. In 13.5 seconds the speedometer would hit 80 mph and in less than a minute the car could be traveling at 115 mph with no sweat at all. What was the lure of such speed outside a race track? Part of it was the new superhighways which had come into being during the Eisenhower term of office. And part of it was the sheer thrill of power. Most people never really attempted to drive their cars 'flat out' anyway. Mostly, there was a deep satisfaction in knowing that if you needed the power, it was there.

Buick celebrated its golden anniversary in 1953. Long known for performance and high quality, the Buick of the 50s was something of the best and the worst of the time.

Buicks of the 50s were big and powerful. Style-wise, they were sometimes rather garish. But, in line with the

Above: Was a car ever painted lavender before the 50s? Here's the Desoto for 1951 in just that color. The women loved it.
Below: Desoto sold only 50,000 cars for the model year 1958. This was due to economic recession as much as anything. The '58 was an extremely fast car.

Top: The 1956 Buick Model 41 Special, a somewhat toned-down model power-wise. Unlike the Century which had 255 hp, the Special boasted a mere 220.

trend toward the fast car, Buick produced its share of exciting automobiles. Most notable of the fast Buicks was the Century. The Buick Century of 1954 came out with a 195 hp V-8 engine coupled with the smaller, lighter body of the Buick Special. It took hardly any time at all for the stock car racers to realize that here was a hot little car capable of scoring big on the tracks. Naturally, General Motors was willing to take advantage of this image. Sales of the Buick were soaring and horsepower was increasing every year.

In 1956, the Buick Special could deliver 220 hp. The Century provided a hairy 255 hp. There wasn't a single Buick built in that year that couldn't exceed 100 mph. The fiery Century could go from 0 to 60 mph in 10.5 seconds and easily exceed 110 mph. By the time the 50s drew to a close, the most powerful Buick featured a 401 cubic-inch (6.6L) V-8 engine with a capacity of 325 hp. But the age of the big over-powered car was fading. In that year, 1959, the little German Opels were capturing an increasing part of the market. The handwriting was on the wall for the enormous power-wagons.

Of all the automobiles still in production today, Oldsmobile is the oldest in the United States. At the turn of the century, people were humming a popular song called, *My Merry Oldsmobile.* The first Oldsmobile was built by Ransom Eli Olds in 1897. It was his amibition to build a car 'in as perfect a manner as possible.' When William Durant formed General Motors in 1908, the infant company absorbed Oldsmobile. But for many years after, the Oldsmobile was still produced by the Olds Motor Works. Not until World War II did Oldsmobile become officially known as the Oldsmobile Division of General Motors. At GM, the Olds led the pack in technological innovation. From the Hydra-matic transmission first introduced on its 1940 models to the overhead Rocket V-8 engine in 1949, Oldsmobile represented the best of GM engineering.

Sherrod Skinner's decision to use the OHV Rocket V-8 in the Olds 88 was nothing short of genius. The 88, which weighed 300 to 500 lbs less than the 98, became one of the outstanding racing cars of the early 50s. Against such formidable contestants as Lincoln, Cadillac and Alfa-Romeo, the Olds 88 proved itself time and again. The horsepower produced by this early Rocket V-8 engine was 165, not bad for a start. But the engineers continued to perfect that engine, following the tenets of RE Olds.

By 1954 the lowest output of an Olds engine was 170 hp. It continued to climb. Two years later, horsepower output for the Olds was 230 and 240. By 1957, you could get an Olds with a special J-2 Rocket engine which had three two-barrel carburetors and 300 horses under the hood. The Olds 88 thus equipped could go from 0 to 60 mph in less than eight seconds. By the end of the 50s, the Super 88 came equipped with a 394 cubic inch (6.9L) V-8 engine, a four-barrel carburetor and a capacity of 315 hp. In the Olds tradition and in the pattern of the times, the car was highly rated for performance and power. Economy was not a strong point, however. And economy was beginning to matter, at least a little.

Chrysler of the early 50s was a rather plain automobile, boxy and not especially stylish, yet Chrysler's engineering was renowned all through the decade. Chrysler had long featured an excellent 6 cylinder engine. But in 1951, Chrysler engineers brought out the hemispherical-head, a very efficient power plant. A hemi could use a lower octane fuel than the non-hemi. Yet the power it produced was equal to any of the conventional engines.

Probably of all the cars produced during the 50s, Chrysler was the most dominant of the powerful cars. The 'lion-hearted Chrysler' was a true description. In 1953, Chrysler's engineering staff had built four special hemis for the Indianapolis 500. All used Hillborn fuel injection and all were capable of developing over 400 hp. Because of a displacement limit, the engineers were never able to realize the full potential of these engines. It was disappointing. Nevertheless, when the Chrysler 300 came out in 1955, it became one of the dominant cars in NASCAR racing, developing a whopping 300 bhp

Top: The pride and joy of an adolescent male growing up in the 50s, this was the ultimate hot rod, lavish with chrome trim and customized paint job.

Bottom: This is something a little more conservative, with regard to paint and chrome, but sure to come off well on the drag strip.

Top: Thunderbird did not long remain the spunky sports car. This four-seater model was introduced in 1958. Ford's venture into producing sports cars was over.

Bottom: The 1958 T-Bird from another angle. Though the Thunderbird is still in production today as a passenger car, many remember the little two-seater fondly.

Top: The dreams of the 50s: a comfortable home and a big powerful car like the 1951 Oldsmobile Super 88 deluxe sedan shown here.

Bottom: A 1959 Olds Super 88 Holiday Sport sedan. Did this proud couple care that their big, roomy Olds, though high on performance, was low in economy? Probably not. No one worried much about fuel economy in those days.

Above: The 1955 Buick Model 46R Special. Buick of the mid-50s were highly successful due in large part to the new 264 V-8 engine.
Following page: A pair of southern belles find the grace and luxury of the '55 Oldsmobile 88 Holiday Coupe exactly to their taste. Even the romantic old South liked to go in style.

from a stock engine. The 1955 Grand National was won by Tim Flock driving the rugged '300' over the notorious Daytona course. Chrysler might have continued to dominate NASCAR racing for many years if the Auto Manufacturers Association had not agreed to downgrade racing.

The production cars were not the only ones dedicated to speed and power. Kids of the 50s with a penchant for tinkering with automobiles experimented with various forms of engines, automobile bodies and frames. In many small towns it was a local pastime to put together a car that would outrun everyone at the track. Such cars were called 'hot rods.'

A favorite combination for the classic hot rod was to match a Model A frame with a body of a 1932 Ford Roadster. For power, a V-8 engine was the thing to have. Added to this was heavy-duty suspension and oversize rear wheels. The roadster, stripped down to bare essentials, looked ungainly and awkward. Each hot rod was a mark of its owner's individualism. No two were ever alike. They were christened with names like the Black Banana, Mongoose, The Plague and Freight Train. They were also extremely noisy, which made the neighbors very irritable.

The kids, of course, could not refrain from 'trying out' these wondrous machines they'd created. So there were clandestine 'drag races' in the wee hours when the streets were deserted. Some didn't even wait for the streets to be deserted, but went rumbling out in broad daylight, just for the thrill of it. The broad streets of Los Angeles, California were particularly attractive for drag racers. The local police frowned on this activity and the participants usually ended up paying a few stiff fines. Still, as the kids argued, working on the cars kept everyone out of worse trouble. No one was robbing little old ladies or pushing dope when he was working on his car.

It was Wally Parks who decided to do something to enable the kids to race safely. Parks founded the National Hot Rod Association in an effort to improve the image of hot rodding and to help the drag racers police themselves. Drag racing became more popular all through the 50s. Like the stock car race, it attracted a varied group of participants. Spectators were mostly the young; kids in their late teens and early twenties. The noise, smoke and smells didn't bother this group at all. It only added to the atmosphere.

The T-Bird was Ford's contribution to the field of speedy cars. The two-seater Thunderbird first came on the scene in the mid-50s. It featured a Y-block V-8 engine of 292 (4.9L) cubic inches. Capable of nearly 200 hp, the Thunderbird was an immediate success both in the showrooms and on the race tracks. Part of the reason was the car's spectacular good looks and the other part was simply its very lively engine.

The car showed its mettle during 'speed week' of 1955. Driven by Bill Spear, the Thunderbird proved the fastest car in Class 3 (cars costing less than $4,000). During this race at Daytona Beach, the T-Bird won over such competitors as the Jaguar 120 and numerous Corvettes.

The two-seater was only in production for three years before Ford's styling department brought out the four passenger model in 1958. It had been a beautiful and exciting small car, but in the 50s it was the big car that piled up sales. Not too many of the big manufacturers were aware of an underground movement toward smaller, more compact cars. But it was underway, a kind of slow groundswell that would hit the market in the 60s. Meanwhile, everyone gloried in a 'bigger is better' concept.

88

Chapter IX. Odd Beasts

There will probably always be that kind of seer, who, when everyone else is buying railroad stock, will be developing low-cost air travel. Powell Crosley Jr was like that. He was an inventive young man. In 1922, he'd become the largest manufacturer of radios in the world. It had all come about through simple innovations which allowed Crosley to produce radios for $20; this at a time when most radios cost $100. From radios Crosley went to refrigerators and was again very successful.

Cars interested Crosley. He had long thought of building a small, low-cost, light-weight economy car. In 1939, he began the first production of such a car in Richmond, Indiana. World War II came along and the factory was forced to shut down. When the War was over, Crosley removed his factory to Cincinnati, Ohio. The Crosley line consisted of a station wagon, a convertible, a sedan, a sports model without doors called the Hot Shot, and another sporty model called the SS which had doors.

They were small. The wheelbase was only 80 inches. The engine was made of stamped sheet metal. The original engine was an overhead cam with four cylinders. It was minuscule 44 cubic inches (0.9L) with a bore and stroke of 2.5 x 2.25 inches. At 5400 rpm, it developed 26.5 hp. The entire engine weight was 60 lbs. Crosleys were the first production cars ever to use disc brakes.

What could have gone wrong for a car that would seem to have so much going for it? Part of it was the times. The U.S. economy was in an upward swing just after World War II. People weren't nearly so interested in small economy cars as they had been during the Depression. They were far more anxious to own a large luxury car. The sheet metal engine, so wondrously light, was also a problem. When the engine was put together it was crimped and spot-welded. Following the spot-welding, it was copper brazed. Electrolysis occurred and the cylinders would look like swiss cheese. It was a very sad situation for a promising little car. To cap it all, the innovative disc brakes rotted away when exposed to road salt.

Crosley took pains to correct all these problems: replacing the sheet metal engine with a conventional engine block and the disc brakes with the standard drum brakes. But the problems had given the Crosley a bad name. Potential buyers turned away in droves. Never mind that the Hot Shot, completely revamped in 1951, won the Index of Performance at Sebring in that year. The car had been given a new 85 inch wheel base. Powered by its new cast iron engine, the Hot Shot could easily do 90 miles an hour. But the buyers were unimpressed. The last Crosley came off the line in 1952, a little car too much ahead of its time.

Bill Frick had long been interested in racing. He was highly impressed with the power of the Cadillac engine. In the late forties, Frick's firm, Frick-Tappet Motors developed a car known as the Fordillac. The Fordillac was a Ford Coupe with a tuned Cadillac V-8 engine. This, harbored in a modified Ford chassis, was what was known as a 'hopped up' special. Bill Frick, who was known for his engine-tuning genius and Ted Tappett, a name used by racing driver, Phil Walters, planned to produce these special models for racing drivers. One of their first customers was Briggs Cunningham, a very well-known race driver. Cunningham was so pleased with the Fordillac that he induced Frick-Tappett to become part of the Cunningham enterprises. Frick-Tappett brought out the Studillac in addition to the Fordillac. The Studillac was a Studebaker Starlight coupled with the Cadillac V-8 and drivetrain. These cars were produced in very limited quantity and were sold mostly to race drivers.

Above: Crosley was certainly a little car ahead of its time. Forty miles on a gallon of gas? One wishes such a car were available today.

Briggs Cunningham (his middle name was appropriately Swift) was a wealthy yachtsman well-known as a participant in the Americas Cup races. He was also deeply interested in auto racing. With the help of one of Buick's chief engineers, Cunningham put together what he called the Bu-Merc. It was a Mercedes-Buick Special, a hopped-up racing car which was driven at the 1940 Worlds Fair Gran Prix and later finished second at Watkins Glen. It was Cunningham's goal to build a car that would finish first at Le Mans.

From 1951 to 1955, Briggs Cunningham became actively involved in the manufacture of automobiles—his own! The prototype for his series was the C-1. It was a good start, sporting in every detail. It rode on a 105 inch wheelbase, was fully instrumented, and upholstered in the finest leather. It was powered by the Chrysler hemihead V-8. In stock form, this engine produced 180 hp. But with careful tuning, Cunningham was able to coax much more from the powerful engine; as much as 300 bhp. The C-2R series followed the prototype and two were entered in the Le Mans in 1951. Both failed to win, however. They were too heavy and the low-octane French gasoline left the powerful hemi-engines knocking.

Most beautiful of the Cunninghams was the C-3, built from 1953-55. This was a grand tourer which used the same tubular frame and suspension as the previous series. The body design was racy and thoroughly Italian, as it was built by Michelotti of the Vignale firm. The only American cars listed of the World's Ten Best Cars in 1953 were the Cunningham C-3 and the Studebaker Starliner. The C-3 sold for 10,000 dollars, a very high-priced car for the times.

1952 saw the advent of yet another series of Cunningham racers. This was the C-4R. The C-4R was 1,000 lbs lighter than the C-2R. It rode on a 100 inch wheelbase and used a 325 hp Chrysler Hemi. Was this the year for America to take the Le Mans? Unfortunately, no. Two of the three C-4R's were forced to drop out. Briggs Cunningham himself drove the other car to fourth place overall, coming in behind two Mercedes Benz racers and a Nash-Healey. He had broken the distance record for the 5 to 8 liter class.

Two of the C-4R's returned to Le Mans for the following year. They were accompanied by the newest model, the C-5R. C-5R was a more sophisticated racer featuring torsion bar suspension, Hallibrand knock-off wheels and Al-Fin brake drums. The same powerful engine breathed under the hood and the car was easily capable of sustained speeds of 150 mph plus. Speed and power, however, are not all that go into a race. Braking ability is just as important and the two D-type Jaguars which came in first and second at Le Mans were equipped with the new disc brakes. The C-5R came in third. The two C-4R's were seventh and tenth.

The last Cunningham was the C-6R which was entered in the Le Mans of 1955. It was nothing like its predecessors, being powered by a 3 liter Offenhauser en-

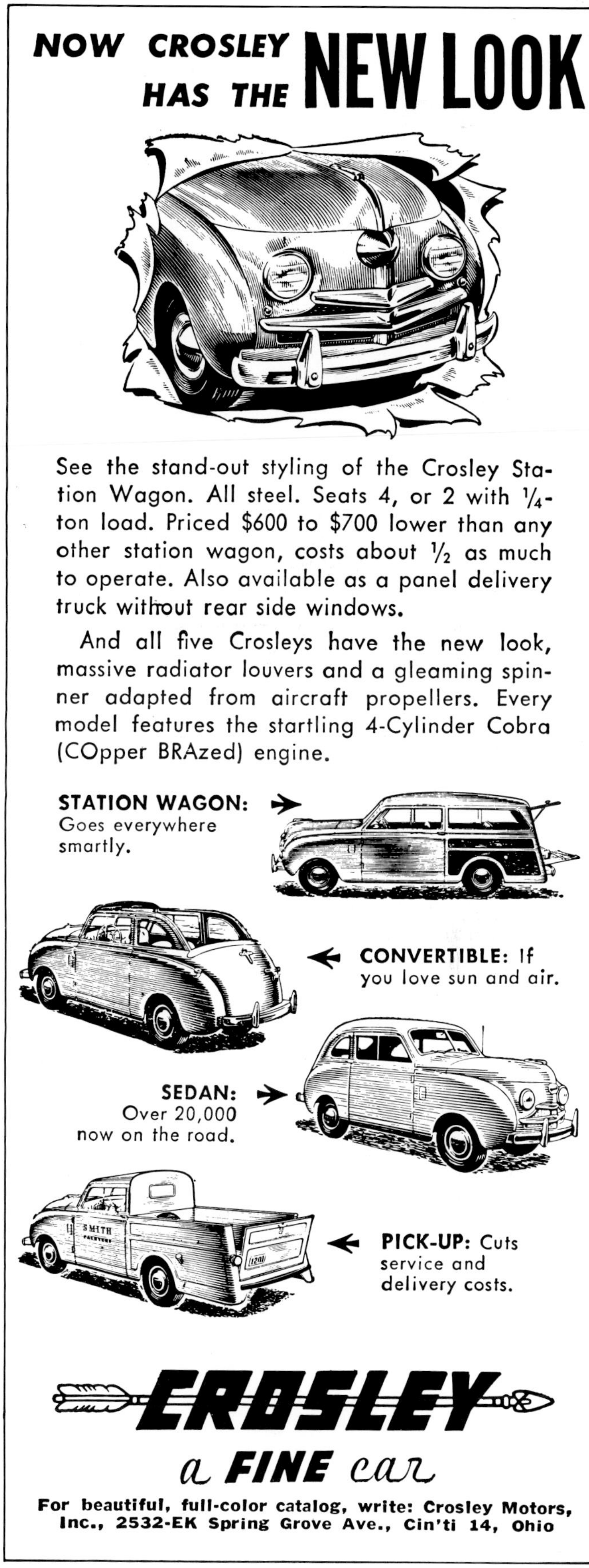

Above: Crosley, one of the strange little cars of the 50s—no chrome, no fins, but a lot of innovation.

Drive the CROSLEY Hotshot

America's own sport car!

Again Crosley makes automotive history—this time with the daring HOTSHOT—a new thrill in motoring! High in style, amazingly low in price—even less than other Crosley passenger models!

The Crosley HOTSHOT follows the dashing lines of racing cars, but will collect a crowd on Main Street or at the club. It's light, fast, economical. For those who want to participate in track racing, road racing or hill climbing competitions, the engine may be souped up as high as 12 or 14 to 1 compression ratio. Also, the windshield, bumpers, top and headlights are removable. Quickly detachable side doors, not shown, as well as top and side curtains, are standard equipment.

Powered by the amazing CIBA (cast iron block) overhead cam shaft engine—the only light, high speed, high compression, racing type engine built in quantity in this country. Equipped with Crosley's revolutionary Hydradisc Brakes—the ultra modern airplane type hydraulic brake now standard equipment on all Crosley cars.

Drive the new Crosley HOTSHOT. Learn about the hundreds of spectacular improvements in the entire Crosley line. For free literature describing the HOTSHOT and the 5 other Crosley models, including Station Wagon illustrated, write Crosley Motors, Inc., 2530-EH Spring Grove Ave., Cincinnati 14, O.

CROSLEY a FINE car

"You See Them Everywhere"

gine. The C-6 had none of the endurance so necessary for the twenty-four hour Le Mans. Briggs Cunningham did not finish. His cars had come so close to winning the Le Mans, but the race rules were against him. Nothing in the United States could compete in the new three-liter category. Cunningham continued racing, but his days of automobile manufacture were over. He had lost over $50,000 a year during the years his cars had been in production.

The King Midget was another of the little cars that came into production just after World War II. The Midget was a two-seater, on a scale with the Crosley. When the Midget first appeared in 1946, it was powered by an 8 ½ hp Wisconsin air-cooled engine and had a manual transmission. The car itself was built of aluminum and steel, with a chassis made of perforated girders and tubing. It was light, and dependable, though more utilitarian than stylish.

In the 50s the cars went to a 9 ¼ hp Kohler engine with an unusual automatic two speed transmission. The simple and dependable transmission consisted of two forward speeds and one reverse. The Midget also featured independent suspension and such optional extras as doors, tops, speedometer, side curtains, golf bag racks, heater, and handcontrols for the handicapped.

Needless to say, the King Midget was not what anyone would call a high volume car. Very few people in the 50s were interested in small compact cars, as we have already noticed. But Midget Motors continued to produce their little car in Athens, Ohio. There were good years, there were bad years. The Midget sold less than 300 cars a year. But they kept on producing and kept on being dependable. Perhaps that is why the Midget survived and so many of the others did not. At any rate, it was one of the strangest of the cars produced in the 50s.

By contrast to other small cars, the Nash Metropolitan was a true success story. George Mason, who was President of Nash Motors, had long engaged in a love affair with small cars. But he was slow and cautious about introducing this love to the public. The first of his small cars had been the Nash Rambler. The Metropolitan was the second.

The Metropolitan was conceived right after World War II. George Mason and his chief engineer, Meade F Moore, chose a design by an independent stylist, Bill Flajole. They built a prototype which was displayed at numerous private showings. This allowed George Mason to wet his finger and see which way the wind blew, in a manner of speaking. The two Georges, Mason and Romney, carefully sized up the market, monitoring public opinion and getting reactions to their small car before going ahead to production.

Though the public seemed favorable, Mason still moved cautiously. By the end of 1953, the Metropolitan went into volume production. Bodies for the little car were built in England by the firm of Fisher and Ludlow of Birmingham. They were then shipped to Austin at Longbridge where the 42 hp engines were installed. The

Opposite: The Crosley Hot Shot deserved more attention than the public gave it. One of the sportiest cars of the times, the Hot Shot was overshadowed by the larger, more powerful cars of the times.
Above: Ads for the King Midget were like the car: miniature.

A-40 was a 4 cylinder engine displacing 73 cubic inches (1.2L). Not exactly in keeping with the times. There was, however, something very appealing about the Metropolitan. Maybe it was the two-toned colors which reminded some of a doubledip ice cream cone. Maybe it was the price tag. The Metropolitan 1200 hardtop which came out in 1954 retailed at 1445 dollars. The little convertible was only 1469 dollars. The Metropolitan, while certainly not speedy in the 50s sense would do a good 70 mph, which was perfectly all right with many people.

Whatever its charm, the Nash Metropolitan began to sell. During late 1953 and 54 nearly 14,000 cars were shipped from Austin.

In 1956 a more powerful Metropolitan 1500 was introduced with an engine displacing 90 cubic inches (1.5L). It did not have the efficiency of a sports car, but that did not matter. Most buyers of the Metropolitans were not looking for sports cars but transportation. Other refinements followed; a real trunk lid, comfortable seats, tubeless tires, and wing vents. By 1959, the price had risen to over 1600 dollars. Sales were at their highest ever—20,435. The Metropolitan of that year ranked second only to Volkswagen among the imports. It was the smallest car of any on the market, having only an 85 inch wheel base.

Chapter X. Duds, Clunkers and the Stillborn

It was described by one comic as 'an Oldsmobile Sucking a lemon.' The Edsel, when it was first being developed in 1955, was Ford's candidate for the burgeoning lower-medium price range automobile. Pontiac, Buick and Dodge had long dominated this market and Ford was eager to get into the action. What happened along the way is proof that nobody, even a large auto company, is immune from mistakes.

In the beginning, nobody could decide on a name for the car that seemed right. The Ford family had not wanted the car to be called the Edsel at all. Poet Marianne Moore, had been requested to help name Ford's new baby. Moore, who'd always had a mischievous side, came up with names like *Utopian Turtletop, Mongoose Civique,* and *Turcotinga.* None of these were particularly inspriring to anyone at Ford Motor Co. Ranger, Pacer, Citation and Corsair were in the top contention, but Ernest Breech, chairman of the board at Ford Motor, didn't like those either. What, after all, was wrong with Edsel? Despite the family's disapproval, Breech managed to have his way and the ill-fated car was dubbed Edsel.

The first Edsel rolled off the production line in 1957. It was not an auspicious year for Edsel's kind of car. The market for low and medium-priced automobiles had just bottomed out. Car sales were in a slump all over. Edsel Division's goal had been to market 100,000 cars for the model year. It produced 54,607 automobiles for the model year 1958. Production dropped drastically during 1958 and only 26,563 Edsels were built. There was a slight rise in 1959 with 29,677 cars coming off the line, but the handwriting was on the wall. The last Edsel drove into the sunset in November 1959.

There were four models in the Edsel line: the Ranger and the Pacer which rode on a 116 or 118 inch wheel base, and the Corsair and the Citation which came on a 124 inch wheelbase. Corsair and Citation came in a line of hardtops, two and four-door sedans, convertibles and station wagons. What is probably most memorable about the Edsel is that strange horse-collar grille, slender horizontal taillights, and some really curious interior devices.

For instance, the Edsel featured 'Teletouch' buttons located in the hub of the steering wheel. These operated the automatic transmission. There was also a revolving drum speedometer, a flaring hood ornament and enormous wraparound bumpers. Edsels came with V-8 engines in a choice of horsepower range. The Ranger and the Pacer came with a 361 cubic inch (5.8L) engine, as did the station wagons from the Corsair and Citation line. For the Corsair and Citation sedans, however, the powerplant was bigger. They featured the 410 cubic inch (6.7L) engine capable of 345 hp. If nothing else, the Edsels were very fast cars. But for the Ford Motor Company they were the biggest mistake of the 50s. Luckily Ford soon recouped its losses.

Kaiser-Fraser Corporation produced some of the most distinctive cars of the 50s. While other cars were big, boxy and heavy, those of the Kaiser-Fraser line were trim, slender models, lighter in weight and with a greater amount of glass area than any other car on the market. Kaiser anticipated Ralph Nader by about fifteen years. Advertising for the 1951 model stressed various built-in safety factors. The Kaiser had a padded dash, recessed instruments, narrower windshield cornerposts, outstanding visibility (due to the large amount of glass). What was a real plus was the windshield which popped out if struck by a force from the interior greater than 35 pounds.

If the styling was unique, so was the engineering. While the Big Three auto companies relied on massive frames, Kaiser engineers John Widman and Ralph Isbrandt built a frame that weighed less than 250 pounds. Despite a lot of head-shaking in other engineering departments, the frame and body combination proved to be extremely rigid. A low center of gravity gave Kaiser excellent handling ability. Perhaps the one drawback to the well-built car was the engine. At a time when nearly every other company had switched to the V-8, Kaiser was still plodding along with the old L-head 6. While the 226 cubic inch (3.7L) L-head was capable of a respectable 115 hp, it didn't begin to compete with other cars of the day.

Kaiser was constantly plagued with left-overs from the previous model year. The beautiful 1951 Kaiser was supposed to have been ready for 1950. Faced with a surplus of 1949 models, Kaiser gave them all 1950 serial numbers and continued to sell them until the stock was depleted. The '51 Kaiser was introduced in March of 1950, six months ahead of time. Sales moved skyward with the introduction. Nearly 140,000 of the 1951 models were sold, in comparison with 15,000 for the 1950

Above: A 1958 Edsel Corsair convertible—something rained on its parade. Edsel was developed to fill the gap for cars in the lower-price range. But before it came off the production line the market had bottomed out. Produced for only three years, from 1957 to 1960, the Edsel is now a collector's item.
Following page: Milady is off to an elegant party in her 1959 Edsel Corsair.

model. Kaiser-Fraser was now 12th in the industry from a lowly 17th the year before.

One of the interesting models that Kaiser offered was the Traveler. Traveler must have been a forerunner of the hatchback, except that it looked like a normal sedan until you opened the hatch. The open hatch revealed a large cargo area and if that wasn't enough, the rear seat could be folded down exactly like a station wagon's. It was an immensely practical car.

Most spectacular of the Kaiser models was the Dragon which first appeared as a series in 1953. The Dragon was distinguished by special goldplated trim on its exterior. The top was padded with a special 'bambu' vinyl, as was the dash and parts of the seats and doors. The seats were upholstered in a special fabric designed by Marie Nichols, famous for fashion design. Every possible option was standard on the Dragon. Such things as tinted glass, Hydra-Matic drive, dual-speaker radio, whitewall tires and the custom carpeting on the floor were just a matter of course when you bought a Dragon. To top it all, there was a gold medallion on the dash to be inscribed with the owner's name. It was a magnificent car, but its price, $3320, kept the buyers away. Only 1277 Dragons were built.

Fraser, the other half of Kaiser, seems, in retrospect, a kind of Siamese twin. The 1950 Fraser, like the 1950 Kaiser, was a left-over '49' model simply used to fill the gap between model changeovers. Fraser offered the usual four-door sedan in the standard series plus a four-door sedan and a convertible in its Manhattan series which was its top line. The convertible was as expensive as a Cadillac and thus not an especially big seller.

The 1951 model changeover at Kaiser left Fraser with the restyled 49-50 Kaiser as its offering for model year 1951. The restyling made the Frasers look dramatically different, however, and they had 50,000 orders for the striking 'new' model. But production of the Fraser was grinding to a halt. As soon as the old Kaiser bodies were used up, the Fraser marque came to an end, leaving many orders unfilled.

Above left: The president and co-founder of Kaiser-Fraser, Henry J Kaiser.
Above right: Edgar Kaiser, brother of Henry, inherited the post left by Joseph Fraser.
Opposite: At a time when other cars were wide and boxy, Kaiser was slim and windswept, a grace other cars would not develop until much later.

Kaiser now prepared to concentrate its efforts on a new small car, the Henry J. Some of the background on this move may be interesting. Kaiser-Fraser had been a thriving young corporation in the late 40s. But from 9th place in the industry, it had declined to 14th and then to 17th. Despite the bleak outlook, Henry Kaiser decided to continue manufacturing cars. This was much against the wishes of his co-founder Joseph Fraser. Fraser left the company as a result of Kaiser's decision. Kaiser borrowed $44 million from the Reconstruction Finance Corporation which allowed him to maintain his inventories and to prepare for the new models. In addition, Kaiser promised his lenders that some of the loan would be used to bring out a small car that everyone could afford to buy new. That car was the Henry J.

Designer Howard 'Dutch' Darrin had proposed a short wheelbase compact similar in line to the elegant 1951 Kaiser. Henry Kaiser wanted something entirely different. What he finally settled on was a little two-door sedan whose prototype had been brought out by American Metal Products, a supplier of frames and springs for car seats. Despite Darrin's efforts to make the car look presentable, it was plainly and simply ugly.

Power for the Henry J came in the form of a Willys-built L-head engine which came in a four and a six cylinder with a displacement of 134 and 161 (2.2 - 2.6L) respectively. The four cylinder model could produce 68 bhp, the six was capable of 80. The admen touted the economy of these cars. As it turned out, the six was something of a hot rod, able to go from 0 to 60 within 14 seconds. Despite its 100 inch wheelbase, the Henry J was a roomy car which could accommodate four passengers and quite a bit of luggage. Its base price was $1363, 200 dollars less than a comparable Chevrolet.

The first Henry J came out in March of 1951. It was enthusiastically received. Almost 82,000 were sold in 1951. But by the end of 1952 the market had bottomed out and sales dropped quickly. Plagued as always by left-over models, Henry J brought out an interim model called the Vagabond. The Vagabond was merely a '51 model with an outside spare tire. This was considered 'continental' styling and it was hoped it would lure buyers into the showroom for a closer look. But the market had been saturated and in 1954, when the last 1100 reserialed 1953 models were finally sold, it was clear that the Henry J was to be a vanished species. Perhaps it was, as many thought, much too austere at a time when the public wanted more luxury. There were many essentials missing from the Henry J: glove boxes and trunk lids to name a few. Other big zeros were its styling and the old-style L-head engine. Like so many small cars in the 50s, it was just ahead of its time.

Kaiser-Fraser Corporation fortunes came to an end in 1955 after 10 years of production and losses of $100 million. The cars had been good ones, but somehow the American public had never warmed to them.

A little-known fact in the history of Kaiser-Fraser is that Sears, Roebuck vice president, Theodore Houser, sat on the Board of Kaiser-Fraser. Houser was eager to market a complete car through the new chain of Sears auto shops which were appearing all across the country

Kaiser's got it...

*Kaiser DeLuxe Club Coupe**

and it's Great!

*Kaiser DeLuxe 4-Door Sedan**

1951 Kaiser

...the only car with Anatomic Design!

Kaiser's got it—exclusive new Anatomic Design—and sales prove that it's the greatest motoring idea in years! Anatomic Design combines styling and engineering to fit your driving needs as no other car has ever done before. Here's what it gives you:

Control-Tower Vision...greatest window area—no "blind spots"! Supersonic Engine...for thrifty High-Torque Power! High-Bridge Doors...curved into roof—no stooping! Tuck-Away Tire Well...for more luggage space! Safety-Cushion Padded Instrument Panel...protection against sudden stops! Level-Flight Springing plus Low Center of Gravity...for a road-hugging, curve-holding ride! Truline Centerpoint Steering...so easy to handle.

See your Kaiser-Frazer dealer now—and try Kaiser's new exclusive Anatomic Ride!

**One of 6 body styles and 12 models.*
Hydra-Matic Drive available in all at extra cost.

Built to Better the Best on the Road!

adjacent to Sears Department stores. Through a special deal with Edgar Kaiser, President of Kaiser-Fraser, Sears brought out the Allstate, a car based on the Henry J.

The first Allstate came out in November of 1951. It had been redesigned by Alex Tremulis and the interior had received a major upgrading. Upholstered in the same heavy duty vinyl used to cover the Atlantic cable, the Allstate featured most of the essentials that the Henry J had scratched. It was an interesting idea; buying a car at a department store. But it failed to catch on. The Allstate was in production for only two years when Sears cancelled the project. The car had been a major mistake for the company. For some years after, the auto parts personnel at Sears would deny the car had ever existed.

Earl Muntz was a prominent business man in the fifties, probably best known in the field of television as 'Mad Man Muntz.' Muntz got into automobile manufacturing when he took over designer Frank Kurtis company, Kurtis Sports Car Corp in Glendale, California. Kurtis had built 36 of his custom made cars when he sold the company to Muntz. The Muntz Jet was a two-door convertible with a 133 hp Cadillac engine. Later, this engine was exchanged for a 205 hp Lincoln V-8 when Muntz moved his factory to Chicago. At the same time, the wheelbase for the jet was extended to 113 inches to accommodate four passengers instead of two. The Jet was an attractive car, lean and clean in its styling, reflecting its heritage as a racing-sports car. It was produced for only five years. But in those five years, they sold all they could build.

By 1960 the American auto industry had reached a kind of maturity. It continued to grow, selling numbers that the pioneers of the industry never dreamed possible. But costs had risen to such heights that it was impossible for new manufacturers to enter the game. From the 1960 on, innovation and new marques would appear as modifications to existing models offered by the 'Big Four.' The Studebakers, Kaisers, Muntzes and the Crosleys had their day and their efforts provide a wonderful reflection on their time.

Above: The 1958 Edsel Pacer, the small Edsel, hoped to appeal to the middle class family on the way up. They were probably more impressed with the lady in mink than the car itself.
Opposite top: The 1958 Edsel Corsair (the big Edsel). Does the somber executive regret his choice?
Opposite bottom: The 1959 Edsel Ranger, another of the small Edsels. This owner obviously didn't care that Edsel's line was being sharply cut back.

Index

Acknowledgements

The publishers wish to thank the following people who contributed to this book: Tom Aylesworth who edited it, Bill Yenne who designed it and the following sources who supplied photographs:

Baird Archives: Pages 148, 151.

Chrysler Corporation: Pages 17 bottom, 20, 45 top, 46 top, 56-57, 60, 61, 62, 63, 68-69, 72-73, 75 bottom, 81, 84-85, 88-89, 92-93, 97 top, 124, 125, 140.

Ford Motor Company: Pages 7, 14-15, 17 top, 24, 26, 27, 28, 29, 32, 34-35, 38-39, 42, 43, 44, 45 bottom, 46-47, 48, 49 bottom, 52-53, 65 top, 80, 104, 105, 108 top, 129 top, 132, 133, 136, 143, 153, 154-155, 158, 159.

General Motors Corporation: Pages 4-5, 8-9, 10-11, 18-19, 21, 22-23, 30-31, 36-37, 40-41, 50-51, 54-55, 58-59, 66-67, 70-71, 74, 76-77, 78-79, 82, 83, 86, 87, 90-91, 102, 102-103, 106-107, 110, 111 bottom, 112 bottom, 118, 119, 129 top, 131, 141, 144, 145, 146-147.

George Hall: Back Cover

Kaiser Corporation: Page 156, 157.

Bev Washburn: Pages 134-135.

San Francisco Public Library: Pages 12-13, 16 top, 33 top, 75 top, 114-115, 126.

World Information Service: 1, 5, 12 left, 33 bottom, 64, 94, 95, 106 111 top, 123, 127, 130, 138, 142, 149, 150.

(c) **Bill Yenne:** Pages 2-3, 25, 65 bottom, 96, 97 bottom, 98-99, 100, 101, 108, 109, 112 top, 113, 116, 117, 121, 128, 137, Front cover.